Up
from
the
Ashes

A Western
Quest Series
Novel

Up
from
the
Ashes

A Western
Quest Series
Novel

Stephen L. Turner

SANTA FE

Sunstone books may be purchased for educational, business, or sales promotional use.
For information please write: Special Markets Department, Sunstone Press,
P.O. Box 2321, Santa Fe, New Mexico 87504-2321.

Book and Cover design ▸ Vicki Ahl
Body typeface ▸ Book Antiqua
Printed on acid free paper

Library of Congress Cataloging-in-Publication Data

Turner, Stephen L., 1957-
  Up from the ashes : a Western Quest series novel / by Stephen L. Turner.
      p. cm. -- (Western Quest series ; 6)
  ISBN 978-0-86534-816-5 (softcover : alk. paper)
  1. Scots-Irish--Texas--Fiction. 2. Reconstruction (U.S. history, 1865-1877)--
Texas--Fiction. I. Title.
  PS3620.U76596U7 2011
  813'.6--dc22

                            2011015774

Published in

WWW.SUNSTONEPRESS.COM
SUNSTONE PRESS / POST OFFICE BOX 2321 / SANTA FE, NM 87504-2321 /USA
(505) 988-4418 / ORDERS ONLY (800) 243-5644 / FAX (505) 988-1025

Dedication

THIS BOOK, AND THE TWO to follow it, is dedicated to the memory of Aaron Lloyd Turner, my great-grandfather. He died in 1939, eighteen years before I was born. I know him only through the eyes and memories of those who knew him, a few photographs, and a rich source of historical documents. His life spanned the American Civil War, the Spanish-American War, World War I, and the early days of what came to be called World War II. He saw the freedom that his forefathers had bought with blood taken away and grudgingly restored. In his youth, the Plains Indians rode unafraid over a vast grassy kingdom populated with millions of buffalo, and as an adult saw both fade away. He was born into a world of muskets and mules which was gradually tied together with steel rails and filled with automobiles and airplanes. He participated in the days of the great cattle drives only to find the trails plowed over and crossed with barbed wire fences. He adapted, changed and persevered. In writing about his life, I have come to know him.

Foreword

THE SACRED SOIL OF TEXAS had hardly been disrupted by Union soldiers during the War of Northern Invasion. Skirmishes and a handful of larger encounters had occurred around Brownsville and the Rio Grande River. There had been a heroic battle at Sabine Pass where a handful of Confederate soldiers and well handled cannon had turned back a Yankee fleet. Galveston Island had fallen briefly into the hands of the Federal navy, only to be driven away until the end of the war. But the interior of Texas had not seen blue-clad armies marching down its roads and ravishing the land.

Tens of thousands of men and boys had marched east to repel the Yankee invasion. One out of four never returned. Many of those who returned did so with broken bodies, and all carried emotional scars that never completely healed.

On June 19, 1865, the heavy boots of victorious Union troops ground ashore at Galveston and spread inland like a plague on the defeated and prostrate state. That day is remembered as "Juneteenth," a day of jubilee for the slaves in Texas. But that day should also be remembered as the day that the boots of those same soldiers began pressing the grapes of wrath in the winepress of Reconstruction.

These tough Texans had seen Mexico throw off the yoke of Spain. Texas had won its independence in a short brutal war with Mexico. After almost a decade as a republic, Texas had finally become part of the United States, only to become embroiled in a bloody war with Mexico to maintain her freedom. Texans had battled Indians, drought, and disease. Nothing had come easily to these resilient people. But what was to come in the long, dark days of Reconstruction would test them to the depths of their souls. Their "never say die" spirit, which had sustained them in the past, would be pushed to its limits.

Acknowledgements

THANKS ARE DUE TO MY dear cousin, Ella Turner Bullard, granddaughter of Aaron Lloyd Turner, for her meticulous research and willingness to share family history. The content of this book has been enriched by the patient editing of my friend, mentor and fellow Texas author, Jim Ainsworth, and the careful proof-reading of my parents, Aaron Lynn and Alene Turner. This series of books, now entering its sixth volume, would not have been possible without the support, encouragement and unending patience of my wife, Roberta.

1

June 5, 1865, Navasota Crossing, Leon County, Texas

"Earth to earth, ashes to ashes, dust to dust."
— Anglican Book of Common Prayer

LIGHTNING FLASHED THROUGH the upstairs window, followed immediately by a deafening deep rumble of thunder. I bolted upright in bed. Disoriented, I looked around the room. Noah was sound asleep in the next bed. With a sigh of relief, I realized it was not Union artillery. A cool wet wind whipped through the open window causing the curtains to flutter. I got up and closed the windows and stood watching the predawn rainstorm. I lay down in bed, listening to rain running off the tile roof and splattering against the glass panes. I had not slept well since returning home. Memories of the past three years interrupted my sleep with nightmares of bloody violence. A few times Noah had gently shaken me awake to remind me the war was over for us. But the war lived on in my darker thoughts and dreams.

I had been a naïve twelve year old boy when I had ridden out with the Texas Fifteenth Cavalry Regiment, Company F, under the Bonnie Blue Flag. I had been seduced by the idea of a great adventure with my older brothers, Noah and David. David had died while we were prisoners in the wretched Camp Stephen Douglas and had been buried in a mass grave in Chicago. Noah and I, along with our brother-in-law, Pink, and our friend, Pecos Wade, had made it home to Texas. I had left a boy and returned a war scarred young man.

I could see the strain of the war on Momma's face. The lines told a story of hardship and sadness. Her joy of our return was tempered by the previously unknown death of David.

I pulled the handmade quilt around me and sank deeper into the cotton mattress. Until a month ago, I hadn't slept in a bed for three years. The quilt smelled like home. The scent of the room, the house, and the plowed fields reminded me I was home. The storm moved on as suddenly as it arrived. The old Rhode Island Red rooster flew to the top rail of the fence to announce the first rays of dawn. I was still a little stiff from all the field work we had done in the last few days and decided to go back to sleep. Within minutes, I heard the clatter of the cast iron stove in the kitchen. As I lay contemplating the coming day, the smell of fresh coffee coaxed me from the warm bed. I dressed quietly, trying not to disturb Noah. I eased down the well worn oak stairs to the kitchen.

"Well, good mornin,' Aaron. You're up early. Did the storm wake you?" Momma gave me a hug and a kiss on the cheek. She tousled my unruly auburn hair.

"I thought the whole Union army was shellin' the house. Glad they weren't."

She touched my face gently. "It's over, son. You're home." She poured us both a cup of strong black coffee. We sat together listening to the fire crackle in the stove. "You boys have worked from dawn to dark since you got back. The fields will be too wet to plow today, so y'all rest."

We had deep plowed sixty acres that had lain fallow for three years. Small saplings, briars, wild blackberries and weeds had grown up in the once tidy fields. The sharp blade of the mould board plow had cut and buried the debris. A spike tooth harrow broke up the clods and a two row lister laid out the furrows. Twenty acres were planted to cotton and another twenty went into corn. The remaining acres were planted to beans, black-eyed peas, potatoes, sweet potatoes, ribbon cane and vegetables. It had been back breaking work and I was glad it was done. The rain was just what we needed.

"You ready for another cup of coffee, son?"

"Are you sure there is plenty?"

"There's enough for now." Jumping up she ran to the stove. "Oh, the cornbread!" She opened the oven door and grabbed the skillet handle with her apron. She cut out a big wedge and set it on my plate. "You do want butter, don't you?"

"Yes, Ma'am, I sure do!" That was the best looking, finest smelling cornbread I could remember. I picked it up to eat with my hands, as the hot butter ran down my fingers and onto the table.

"Aaron Lloyd Turner! Where are your manners?" She smiled as she said it.

"Sorry, Momma, I couldn't wait for it to cool. Now that is what I call cornbread!" Flattery and my dimples had saved me again.

"We got all the eggs we can eat. How many do you want and how do you want them cooked?"

"Five, fried, please."

While the eggs cooked, she carved off thick slices of smoked bacon into another skillet. The aroma of the frying bacon and eggs, mixed with the smell of the hot cornbread and coffee warmed my heart and made me smile. It was good to be home.

Momma sat down at the table Logan Morgan had made for her and watched me eat. "It's so good to have you and Noah here. I like your friend, Pecos. He fits right in with the rest of us. I'm so glad Pink made it home to be with Mary Ann. I'm still grieving over David, God bless him, and Alma, too. Raising Alice has been a handful, but she is good company for me. I have been waiting to tell you. You lost a half-brother, too. A Confederate deserter shot and killed Lucius while robbing his store over in Groesbeck. Ilene took the children to live with her family down on the Leon River."

Lucius, Marcus and Louisa King were Mother's children from

her first marriage. Her husband had died in the War of 1812. After they had married, Father had raised her children as his own. Louisa had died of cholera a few years back. Of Mother's ten children, only Marcus, Noah, Mary Ann and I survived. They say Texas is heaven for men and cattle, but is hell on women and horses.

———————————

I caught a bay gelding with the intention of riding our boundary fences to see what neededrepairs. The horse was a little snuffy when I climbed on. With a snort and a squeal he hunched his back and crow hopped across the corral. I pulled his head around to the left and hooked him with my left spur causing him to turn in a tight left hand circle. I let the pressure off his head and spurred him into a lope. He continued to buck a little as I kept running him in a wide circle hoping he would remember why God made horses. By the time he was starting to lather up, I eased him into a walk to let him cool off. When he was calm, I stepped down off him and loosened the cinches so he could blow. I talked a little Texan to him and retightened the saddle. I patted on his neck a bit, and then stepped up on him. This time he was a lot more neighborly. I put him into a long trot headed south until we struck the main road, the famous Camino Real. After a short run west, we headed north along the river road. He turned out to be a good responsive horse. I was enjoying the ride. The saddle leather creaked and groaned as we travelled the shady road with the forest along the Navasota River on the left and our homestead on the right.

My father, Aaron Turner, had been granted a league and a labor from Spain by the alcalde of Nacogdoches. He had to re-file his claim when Mexico obtained its freedom from Spain in 1820. When Texas won its independence from Mexico in 1836, the General Land Office of the Republic of Texas had confirmed his title to the four thousand six hundred acres. He had fought in the Texas Revolution, and had been called to duty as Colonel of Scouts when Mexico had declared war on the United States because of the annexation of Texas. Father had died the day after my first birthday. All I knew about him was what my mother, brothers and sisters had told me. My oldest brother, David, had been the closest thing I had to a father, even though he had only been eight years older than me. He had died of pneumonia while we were prisoners of war in Camp Stephen Douglas in Chicago. I still missed him. His death had broken one of the few ties I had to Father. But this land had been his. He had fought bandits, Mexicans and Indians to keep it. He was buried here and I thought sometimes that I could feel him near me.

I found the fences needed some repair, but nothing major. I came to the small creek that angled from northeast to southwest that marked the irregular north boundary of our property. The fence here was built above the flood plain of the stream. It was in good shape.

I took time while I was on the north pasture to ride through our herd of crossbred cattle. Father had imported a Shorthorn bull to upgrade the native longhorns. Much of our herd was three-quarters Shorthorn breeding. Few cattle had been sold during the war. My half-brother, Marcus King, had come over from Limestone County to do the branding and castrate the bull calves each spring. He had left a few of the most promising looking calves as bulls; they were now breeding age. The steers were two and three years old, fat and market ready. That gave me an idea I wanted to pitch to Noah and Pecos.

Our horse herd had been kept in good condition. A few three-quarter blood Thoroughbred stallions had been held back to breed to our good crossbred mares. The colts had been gelded each year in the fall before they became two years old, and they had been halter broke along with the fillies. Although Noah and I did our part, Pecos was the top hand when it came to training horses. Before too long, all the geldings and some of the better fillies were broke to ride. The pastures were in great shape and could carry much more stock than we owned.

The Spanish jack had died of colic during the war. Thankfully, there were no young mules to train. They were a lot harder to work with than the horses. The mules we had left behind had been used some to keep them gentle; there were enough of them to do all the work. Mamma had kept them hidden in the river bottoms when the Confederate resupply agents came through.

As I resumed my ride along the north boundary, I came to the site where the brewery and distillery had been. Mother had said a fire had started around one of the copper pots and quickly spread through the wooden buildings. The intense heat of the fire had killed the ground. All that was left were heaps of thick dark gray ashes. The wet piles gave off a strong odor in my nose and throat. The family who had owned it and all the families who worked there had moved away.

Turning south, I followed the east boundary all the way to the Camino Real. What stories, what history had this road seen? You wouldn't know it to look at it, it had been the most important road in Texas in its day, but that day was rapidly passing away. Armies, Texas Rangers, Indian war bands, and hordes of settlers no longer pounded its ancient rutted surface.

Across the road I could see smoke curling from the chimneys of the cabins belonging to Logan Morgan and Sheriff Tanner Moore. Logan still worked as a carpenter and Tanner was now the deputy sheriff, as the county seat had moved to Centerville where the Leon County Sheriff lived. I didn't stop to visit. I had too much on my mind.

The bay gelding loped west along the road toward Navasota Landing. I reined him in to survey what had been a thriving prosperous community before the war. It was a forlorn sight. Mother's store was still in good repair, but only open part of the time. It didn't matter too much anyway. There was hardly anything to sell or trade. The school and the church stood silent and unused, in need of repairs. The doctor was gone, as were both lawyers. The war had claimed the lives of all three. The inn had been torn down, salvaged for the lumber. Sheriff Moore's small office was still in use when he was there. He did a little gun repair from his office, too. There was a blacksmith's shop to serve the remaining farmers and residents, but it looked none too prosperous. The bells from the school, the church tower and our cabin were all gone, taken to forge cannon somewhere far away. The skeleton of a community was silent and ghostly. No children's voices came from the school. There wasn't a single horse or wagon tied up along the once thriving street. No dogs lounged under the porches and no chickens scratched in the road.

The Navasota River was running high this morning from the storm. The ferry floated attached to a series of pulleys that could be worked from either bank. I remembered Mother telling me how the ferry had carried people and animals continuously for days during the "Runaway Scrape" of 1836. I followed the river road south. The pottery works, tannery, saddle shop and the cabins of their owners were all gone. The tanning pits were all that remained. It looked as if the river had gotten out of its banks and washed them all away.

I took a seldom used side trail back north and found the old Teel farm. The main cabin stood vacant, but the barn, outbuildings and one small cabin looked like they were being used. There were hogs in a pen, an early garden, and chickens scratching around the small tidy cabin. I saw an elderly black man with white hair and wearing faded bib overalls drawing water at the well.

"Tysoe! It's Aaron Turner!"

"As I live an' breathe it is. Massa Aaron, it sho is good to see ya. Glad ya tol' me who ya was, cause you growed plenty while you been gone. I heared you and Massa Noah came home safe. I sho am sorry about yo' brother. Massa David was a good man. I wuz da one dat dug da grave fo' his wife, Miss Alma, when she passed. Yo Momma been raisin' that po' chil' all by herself."

I didn't know how old Tysoe was. Cody Teel had won him in a horse race over forty years ago and set him free. He had worked for them as a farm hand ever since.

"Da Teel fambly been gone a long time. Dey moved out west and left me here to watch things. I ain't heared a word in a long time, I doan eben know if dey still alive. But I manage here pretty good by myself."

"You never married?"

"Now who would have a worn out ol' darkie like me? I'm usta stayin' by myself. Won't ya get down and eat a bite of vittles? I got some squirrel stew?"

"No. Thanks anyway. I need to get on home."

"Sho ain't much left of town no how. Like da preacher say,

'Ashes to ashes, dust to dust. The Lord gives and da Lord takes away.'
He been mostly takin' away from here fo' a long time."

When I reached the Camino Real I took one last look around.
Tysoe was right. 'Ashes to ashes, dust to dust.'"

_____

In May, the last battle in the War Between the States had occurred in and around Palmetto Ranch and Brownsville, Texas. Colonel
John "Ol' Rip" Ford had driven a Yankee force back to their base
with only the loss of few lives, and a few embarrassed Yankees were
captured and released. On May 26, the Confederate high command
in Texas had met and agreed to surrender all remaining forces. They
were to lay down their arms and go home or surrender to the first
Union forces they encountered.

Confederate Brigadier General Joseph Shelby of Missouri
refused the order, claiming the Texans had no authority to command his brigade of over a thousand cavalry troopers. They found
the Confederate arsenal at Waco unguarded and helped themselves
to uniforms, supplies, new rifled muskets and ammunition, and ten
brand new howitzers. They boldly rode across Texas and crossed into
a self-imposed exile in Mexico July 1.

At the same time, Federal warships docked in Galveston Bay,
unloading thousands of Union troops. They were mostly colored
troops under white officers, sent especially to Texas to emphasize that
the war was over and slavery was abolished. A decree was sent out by
Yankee General Gordon on June 19, 1865, announcing that all slaves in
Texas were immediately and forever free.

There were now 200,000 newly freed slaves in Texas with
nowhere to go, nothing to do and no guidance. There was no place
to call home, no jobs, and no way to feed them. Many flocked to the
larger cities where no provision for their care had been anticipated.
Some aimlessly wandered the countryside, and some just kept working in the fields and living in their slave cabins, for they had nowhere
else to go. No one had considered what would happen to these men,
women and children. When Moses freed the children of Israel, God

fed them manna from heaven. When the conquerors of the South freed the slaves, they got to vote, serve on juries, and hold public office. They would have to find food, jobs, and shelter on their own.

We had all sworn an Oath of Allegiance to the United States when we had surrendered as a condition of our parole. We swore an oath that we would never again take up arms against the United States. It had been enough.

Andrew Johnson had become President of the United States when Abraham Lincoln had been struck down by John Wilkes Booth. He implemented a policy of amnesty for former Confederates who had taken the Oath of Allegiance. It was hoped that they would peacefully return home and work to feed their families. His policy of Reconstruction was based on three simple points: the abolition of slavery, the repudiation of secession, and the disavowal of all Confederate debts. It gave us hope that there would be a rapid healing of the wounds of war and a return to normalcy.

Sadly, it was not to be. Federal troops had never been successful in invading Texas' sacred soil. Their conquering boots now setting foot in Texas would soon begin treading the winepress of the grapes of wrath.

2

Farewell to Farming

"I'M TIRED. I'M TIRED."
Alice whined on the wagon seat next to me.

"Shush, now, Alice. We're almost there." I could hear a hint of strain in Momma's voice. I slapped the reins across the mules' backs to squeeze out a little more speed. I think they were getting tired of listening to Alice, too. Marcus had moved from Personville to Groesbeck during the war. Pink and Mary Ann lived there, too. It would be the first time we had all been together since before the war.

"Well, look at that, Aaron, Groesbeck four miles! Are the mules fresh enough to trot that far?"

"I reckon they are, but it will bounce the wagon around some."

Momma grabbed the long whip and let out a crack and a yell that set those mules into a nice long trot. "I'm plum worn out from wrestling with Alice." The wagon lurched forward, raising a cloud of dust. Noah and Pecos kicked their horses to keep up.

Marcus and his wife, Glynna, had a nice frame house on the edge of town. He ran a saloon of the better sort in Groesbeck where respectable men could get a drink and a little peace and quiet. We had a nice supper of fried chicken, mashed potatoes, gravy and biscuits. Marcus produced a bottle of good aged Kentucky bourbon after supper. The glasses had just been finished when the lamps of a buggy pulled into the yard. A gray-haired man in a Confederate officer's frock coat stepped down.

Pink recognized him first. "Captain Tyus!"

We bolted out the door to greet our former commander and treasured friend. He looked up with a sparkle in his blue eyes. "Aaron, Noah, Pink and Pecos! The entirety of my former command." From long habit, we saluted, which he briskly returned. "Thank you for inviting me, Marcus. This is wonderful."

We sat in the front room catching up on the news since our parole. He owned land in Leon, Limestone and McLennan Counties, but lived near Waco. "My slaves are all gone. There is no one to work the fields. I suppose my days as a cotton planter are about over. But, I have my law practice and my livestock. We'll manage fine. I want to talk to you about a way we can earn hard cash for the lean days ahead."

I glanced at Noah and Pecos. I suspected his idea was similar to what I had mentioned to them.

"We haven't marketed enough cattle during the war to buy coffee. I have steers in my herd that are two to four year old prime beef. Around here, they bring three to five dollars a head, mostly for the hides and tallow. The Yankees are extremely short on beef. Grown steers bring thirty or more dollars a head." We smiled as we began to understand what he was proposing.

"There are thousands of cattle that are unclaimed and unbranded. They have wandered wherever green grass has drawn them. The cane breaks, thickets and river bottoms are full of them, free to any man with the will to rope and brand them. I propose that we put together a herd to drive up the Shawnee Trail to Sedalia, Missouri next June. I think it would take about three months to get them there."

"Would you lead the drive, Captain Tyus?" I asked.

"No, my place is here. Events will be happening in Texas which will require my presence. I'll help organize things, but I had planned for the four of you to be in charge."

Noah glanced at Momma, then back at him. "Sir, I've spent too much time away from Mother. I'll help put the drive together, but I'm not going."

"Same, here, Cap. I neglected Mary Ann all through the war. I'm staying here with her."

Captain Tyus nodded his understanding. "Aaron? Pecos?"

"A regiment of Yankees couldn't keep me from goin'. I never did care much for farmin' anyway."

"Same, here, Cap! Count me in."

We planned and cussed and discussed late into the night. It was a thing we could do. Come June 1, 1866, we would push whatever stock we had put together to the Tyus place on the Brazos. There was much to be done.

We repaired and replaced missing rails on the perimeter fence. The sound of axes rang in the woods outside the pastures. Post oak trees were cut for replacements. Pecos designed a special corral for holding any wild cattle we might catch until they were a little more civilized. "It needs to be round to keep 'em from bunchin' up in the corners, and eight feet high. I've seen longhorns down on the Colorado where I was raised clear a six foot fence with room to spare. It's gonna have to be so tight they can't squeeze through, and so strong they can't even put a dent in it. Horse high, bull strong and pig tight."

We sawed, cut and dug from daylight to dark until it was finished. It looked more like a fort than a corral. Heavy gates swung on iron hinges salvaged from a steamboat. We had rigged a hand pump to fill water barrels on the inside. It was as good as the three of us could make it.

Just as we finished, a stranger rode up on a dapple gray gelding of good breeding. He wore a Confederate private's uniform and a slouch hat. There was a brace of pistols draped across the saddle. He led a pack horse carrying panniers.

"You boys built quite a fort. When you gonna mount the cannon?" He grinned and looked us over cautiously.

"We need a real sturdy corral for catchin' maverick cattle. My name's Aaron Turner. Get down and water your stock. We got some corn pone and a jug of spring water, if you want some. This is my brother, Noah, and my friend, Pecos Wade."

"Shelby. Just plain Shelby."

"We were with the Texas Fifteenth, mostly in Tennessee and Georgia. How about you?"

"I didn't say. Here and there."

Pecos reached to pick up a shotgun, but before he could raise it Shelby's gun was out and cocked. "Put down the scatter gun, Rooster. If I was aimin' to rob or hurt ya, you'd already be dead. I'm tired, hungry and broke. I'm lookin' for a place to earn my keep. Can you use a good cowhand?"

"That depends on you. We don't take too kindly to bein' drawed on."

He holstered the gun and climbed down. He was over six feet tall with dark brown curly hair and clean shaven. He had gray eyes that looked right through a man, but a crooked smile and dimples to soften the effect. "Sorry about that. I peeled off from General Joseph Shelby's column when they were in Waco. I didn't want to ride off to Mexico with 'em. I been dodgin' them slow-witted colored troops ever since. Who's the boss?"

"That would be Aaron." Noah said flatly.

"Why, you look like the youngest! You think you can boss an outfit?"

"I've had plenty of Yankees try to kill me, an' I killed my share. Noah and Pecos put me up for boss. If you don't wanna work for me, you can crawl back in whatever hole you crawled out of. You get out of line, you might die o' lead poisonin'."

"Y'all sure are a bunch of sore heads, but I'll give it a try. If I can't hold up my end, you don't owe me nothin'." He held out a strong hand. I reluctantly shook it. The time would come when I would regret it.

———

The campfire crackled and hissed as we talked and finished our coffee. It reminded me of all the nights we had sat together during the war. Shelby didn't say much. He mostly kept to himself, but always had a gun close at hand.

"You expectin' trouble?" Pecos goaded him.

"Not unless you plan to start some."

Pecos looked at us and shrugged. "Where'd you serve?"

"Prairie Grove and Pea Ridge in Arkansas, then around some."

"What unit?"

"I didn't say. Mostly on detached duty."

"Sounds to me like you gone and detached yourself."

Shelby's eyes flared at Pecos. "I ain't no deserter! My business is my own unless you feel big enough to make it yours."

"We got enough work to do tomorrow without y'all fightin' tonight. Just hush up and get some sleep." I growled. Neither seemed interested in pushing the issue, but I knew the two would lock horns someday soon.

———

The brush exploded in crashing branches and bawling cattle in the thicket along the creek. An old longhorn bull, four cows and three calves charged headlong through the dry fall debris. The bull broke from cover first. He was a mealy nosed brown bull with a few white spots on the rump. Noah had his horse right on him. He settled a rawhide loop over the wide horns. The thick eight strand braided riata pulled tightly closed around his upturned horns as Noah dallied to the saddle horn. When the bull jerked the slack out of the rope, it slammed him hard to the ground. He jumped up and charged straight at Noah and his horse. Spurs urged the horse into action. He swung wide to throw the bull off balance. I charged in on my horse and roped his back feet. I gathered slack and stretched the bull out until he hit the ground with a thud. With his horse holding tension on the rope, Noah climbed down and tied the bull's back feet with a strong short rope. He managed to get a double wrap around his front legs, and the old fighter was secure. Once it was safe, we retrieved our ropes and took out after the cows and calves still in the thicket.

Pecos and Shelby had similar luck across the creek. They had caught a spotted cow and calf. Both were tied on the ground. The other two cows headed down the brush along the creek. We caught the cow with the calf and tied them down. Noah and Pecos caught the other one. She was old, barren and fat; perfect for the market.

We built a small fire and branded the cow, her heifer calf, and the old bull with a Rafter T on the left hip, and an upside down T over the left ribs, our agreed road brand. We castrated the old bull, changing him into a stag, and left all of them tied. We used a short handled shovel and carried hot coals across the creek to start a fire to brand the cattle Pecos and Shelby had caught. The bull was castrated and all of them were branded and ready for Missouri.

We had bought a string of eight gentle work oxen for nearly nothing from Logan Morgan. They had been left back at our camp. Shelby rode back to get them. With great care and difficulty, we yoked the adult longhorns to the oxen. The wild cattle never missed an opportunity to try to kill us, but the oxen held them back. The oxen stubbornly held their ground and leaned against the wild cattle to impose their will. The calves trotted along noisily beside their mothers as they plodded slowly back to our camp. The oxen dragged the longhorns to water. They were thirsty enough that they submitted meekly to drink.

We left them yoked to graze as we returned to find another bull and two cows. We soon had them branded and yoked to the other oxen. Following the cows was one pretty little heifer calf and one bull calf, which we castrated. For our first day's work, we had two stags, one barren market cow, four good breeding cows, three heifer calves and two little steers. We drove them slowly back to the home pasture and left them yoked together until they were a little calmer. It was a good start.

We continued to work the upper reaches of Boggy Creek for two more weeks. Due to the limited number of oxen, we were only able to bring in eight adult animals per trip, not counting calves at side. Once we were within ten or twelve miles from our home pasture we adopted a different tactic. Two of us rode on either side of the creek and drove the cattle ahead of us. They mostly tried to stay in the thickets, but if they broke for the prairie we turned them back into the creek bottom. Our drive produced squealing wild hogs, countless deer, a few coyotes, armadillos, possums, and one unhappy little skunk.

We had taken down a wide span of rail fence nearest the creek. Once we got close to the fence, we drove the wild cattle out of the creek bottom and toward the open prairie where our oxen grazed quietly. We slowly kept the longhorns headed in the right direction. Soon their natural curiosity attracted them to the oxen. Once they had entered the large pasture, we replaced the rails. We caught seventeen bulls, a barren cow, and thirty young breeding age cows with twenty five calves. We branded everything and castrated the bulls. Soon, they were mixed into our main herd. One stag kept tearing his way through the fence. Two of us would rope him and drag him back bawling and snorting to the pasture. After a week of this, we grew tired of playing this game and decided he would be better as jerky than for trailing to Sedalia. The meat was a little tough, but a whole lot less trouble than fixing fence.

3

Mavericks and Swamp Angels

"BOYS, I THINK WE GOT ALL the wild cattle worth catchin' along Boggy Creek. It's time we start workin' the Navasota."

"Aaron, who died and made you king?" Noah snarled.

"We already talked about this. If you want to start this all over, let's get it done."

"You brothers stick a sock in it. We got work to do." Pecos flashed an ornery grin.

The heavy breath of the oxen left clouds of steam in the early morning air. We had a pack mule with us carrying our soogans and groceries. We slowly travelled eight miles or so in about two hours. The oxen were not famous for their speed.

My horse pointed his ears at the forest along the river. A glimpse of cattle was barely visible disappearing into the brush. We tied up the pack mule and left the oxen to graze. We fanned out heading south. The crash of large animals breaking through the dry underbrush echoed along the Navasota.

27

"Slow down. We don't want 'em to try to swim the river." We reined up to a slow trot. I eased out onto the edge of the prairie along the edge of the woods. So far the cattle were holding in the thicket. "Go slow. I'll be back."

I headed my horse out of the thicket and on to the river road. Once there, I spurred him to a gallop until I reached the northwest corner of our land. I tore down fifty yards of rail fence and hastily rebuilt it from the river across the woods to the corner of our fence. With any luck, the wing fence would divert the cattle from the thicket and onto our pasture. I just should have thought of it sooner.

I rode back and caught up with the others. "I made a big hole in our fence and used it to build a wing fence to turn 'em out of the river bottom. If we take it real easy it may work, if we chouse 'em, they'll jump over it and be gone."

The crashing in the brush grew louder as the number of cattle we were pushing continued to grow. Bulls were bellowing, cows were bawling and calves were squalling for their mothers. I swung out wide and got ahead of the cattle. My horse was snorting and prancing with excitement. As Pecos, Noah and Shelby eased up behind them, the cattle began to leave the safety of the river bottom for the open prairie. When they saw me, they turned south along the river road. An old brindle cow was the first to encounter the wing fence. She sniffed it and turned to follow it into the pasture. A tight bunch of mixed cattle crowded behind her through the gap in the fence and onto our land. Pecos went back for the pack mule and the oxen while the rest of us started putting the fence back up and let the horses cool off. The cattle continued to follow fences until they were at the east boundary fence almost three miles away.

"I'm tired and hungry. I hope that good for nothin' half-breed Injun gets back here with the pack horse pretty soon." Shelby complained.

"He don't make any secret about bein' part Comanche. But he's all man, and my friend. You best learn some manners."

"Pecos served with us for three years in the war. He's like family. Maybe you ought to listen to Aaron."

Shelby just shrugged and went back to work. Noah and I rode

over to get a head count on the cattle and left him to finish the fence. We counted one hundred twenty-seven adult cattle and forty or fifty calves. We couldn't get close enough for a better count. We would sort, brand and castrate those that needed it later. As we rode back, we spotted the oxen plodding across the grass toward the longhorns. They would help them settle down.

When we got back, Pecos was sitting in the shade eating cold cornbread, but Shelby was stretched out flat on the ground. "He asleep?"

"Nope. Hit his head."

I noticed a red swollen place on Pecos' cheek and the skinned knuckles of his left hand. I tied my horse and walked over for a closer look. I nudged Shelby with my toe, but he just groaned. Noah rolled him over on his back to discover Shelby's face looked like it had been hit with a whole nest of hornets. The revolver he always carried was on the ground near the road. We doused him down with a little water. His eyes jerked open. "Where's my gun?"

I removed each of the percussion caps before handing it to Shelby. "What's your story? Pecos said you hit your head."

Shelby stared at his hands. "I fell and hit my head."

Pecos shrugged and passed the cornbread. Whatever had happened or been said, it never came up again.

———

Our last gather was on the Navasota south of the crossing. We set up camp about ten miles north of where the Navasota runs into the Brazos. Deer edged out of the woods to nibble rye grass in the meadow at dusk and the coyotes started singing just at dark. The sky was clear, crisp and cold. Cattle were bawling in the thicket. Tomorrow promised to be a productive day.

We took the oxen and pack mule part of the way with us and left them where there was good grass and water. We put hobbles on the mule to keep him from straying too far. The horses seemed to sense the presence of cattle. Their ears were alert and they pranced in excitement. We plunged into the brush. All of us were wearing chaps to protect our legs from the brush, as it was the densest we had worked yet. It wasn't going to be easy. A deer bounced away at our approach as did a couple of hogs and an armadillo. We could hear cattle ahead of us.

"Ain't no way to throw a rope in this mess. We're gonna have to push 'em out in the open." Before these words were out of my mouth, an old longhorn cow with a young calf jumped up from a tangle of briars and charged straight at my horse. The tone of her bellow carried a message of deadly intent. I wheeled the bay to the right and set spurs to get him moving. He didn't need any encouragement. It was obvious the old critter had murder on her mind.

She caught my horse a glancing blow with her up curved left horn, slicing him open across the right hip. He squealed in pain and bolted for the safety of the open prairie, as I held on for dear life. The old brute stopped with her calf behind her and tossed dirt over her back with her horns. I had just gotten my horse under control when she charged again. The bay wheeled his injured rump out of the way just in time for me to toss a wide loop over her horns. It settled down perfectly as I raced the horse to gather slack out of the rope. I now found myself dallied to a very angry cow with a bad attitude and a notion to kill me. The sudden loss of slack jerked her hard around, facing me with rolling eyes and slinging snot. She wobbled at the end of the stout rawhide rope until her eyes slowly came back into menacing focus. With a snort, she charged again. I galloped the horse in a sweeping right-hand circle, barely managing to keep her from climbing up the rope.

Pecos came barreling out of the brush with a loop in his hand. His first throw caught her by both hind feet. She went down hard when she hit the end of Pecos' rope. We squared up so that we had her stretched out between us. Noah jumped off his horse and tied her back feet with a heavy pigging string.

"Y'all keep her stretched out tight or I'm gonna git killed!" He eased forward and managed to get both of her flailing front feet pulled together and secured with a double loop. Once she was tightly tied, we let slack in our ropes and Noah flipped the loops off her horns and feet. She continued to thrash about on the ground until Shelby arrived carrying her calf. Once the calf was near enough to lick, she calmed down enough so that we could have a look at her.

Noah grimaced and motioned for me. "Look, a notch on her left ear."

With some fear and difficulty we rolled her over to see her left hip. Plain as day she was branded TM 45.

"Aaron, whose mark and brand is that?" Pecos groused.

"I know. I've seen it for years. Tanner Moore."

"Our friend, the sheriff. Hey, little brother, wonder why she has a 45 branded on there?"

"Betcha that was the year she was branded!" We fell out laughing. We had nearly gotten ourselves killed by a twenty year old cow that belonged to somebody else!

Once we had enough cattle caught to lead back with the oxen, we gathered up the sheriff's cow, too. We left them yoked to the oxen over night for the drive back home the next morning.

The sheriff grinned when he saw her. "Well, I'll be. I never thought I'd see her again. She's been trouble since she was just a heifer. Tell you the truth, I was kinda glad she was gone. If you boys want her, she's yours for nothin'." We weren't sure if she was more of a gift or a curse, but we thanked him and took her home anyway.

The cut on the bay just needed to be washed out and treated with a little bacon grease. All the horses were pretty tired from our ordeal, so we gathered up fresh ones and started out for another round of catching wild cattle. It wouldn't hurt my feelings if they were just a little less wild. By midday we were back in the breaks again. Soon we were on a nice bunch of mostly bulls which we pushed out onto the prairie to rope. We caught eight without too much trouble and yoked them to the oxen. We drove the uncaught animals back into the river bottom with the hope we could get another shot at them later.

After a supper of fried bacon and cornbread, we were getting settled in for a much needed night's rest. The day had been hot, but it was cooling off quickly. As Pecos started to unroll his soogans, Shelby jumped up close to him with his pistol drawn.

"Don't move!" Before we understood what was happening, he fired. He holstered his pistol and stepped over Pecos' bedroll and flipped out his knife. In a flash he cut the head off the biggest cane-brake rattler I had ever seen. Holding it up above his head, there was still a good foot and fifteen rattles on the ground. We guessed it was close to eight feet long and over seventy pounds.

"Thanks, Shelby." Pecos offered a shaking hand.

Shelby ignored the out-stretched hand and wiped the knife off on his sleeve. "I'd have done the same thing for a damn Yankee."

We continued to rope and gather this way until we had worked close enough that it would be possible to attempt to simply drive what animals were left onto our place. We opened up the rail fence and used the rails to make a temporary wing fence as we had done before. At least this time we had planned ahead. We tied two hemp cords across the Camino Real to keep the cattle from turning back east. White rags were tied to the twine about every four feet. It wouldn't stop a rabbit, but we hoped it would direct the cattle where we wanted them to go.

When everything was ready, we hit the river bottom south of the road about daylight. Sheriff Moore and Mr. Morgan agreed to ride with us out on the prairie to keep the cattle from making a run for it. The brush along the river was working alive with cattle. We rode popping our chaps and hollering. The brush ahead of us shook with the movement of a large bunch of cattle. We had heard a few yells from out on the flanking prairie, but the cattle for the most part held tight to the brush. When the first longhorns got to the end of the woods, they saw our gentle oxen grazing peacefully across the road. The decoys worked like a charm and the wild brutes were drawn in by their tamer cousins. A few challenged the string fence, but the flapping white rags turned them back with a snort.

The last of the wild cattle were loping into the pasture when one young bull decided to turn back. He followed the string fence until he came to the end of it at the front porch of the store. He neatly jumped up onto the porch and stopped dead in his tracks. He was standing on a wooden floor for the only time in his life. He picked up and set down his feet as if he was walking through a den of snakes. The big heavy door was standing wide open. He trotted right through the door like he owned the place. Momma and little Alice were in the store. Mother grabbed a broom and came charging after the bull.

"Git out of here, you spotted devil!" she swatted him across the rump with the broom. This startled the bewildered bull which promptly lunged into a shelf of canned goods causing it to fall over with a clatter. This seemed to excite him somewhat. He began to run in circles around the store, bellowing and slinging snot in every direction. He finally realized his only escape from the crazy woman with the broom was through the open door. Finding freedom, he stuck his tail up in the air, promptly ran across the road, jumped the rail fence and rejoined his friends. The store looked like a manure wagon had exploded inside. Cornmeal, flour and canned goods were scattered everywhere. When I came through the door, Momma and Alice screamed. I had to duck a swat from the broom.

"Whoa, Momma! It's me!"

Looking at the mess, I broke up laughing. Then she hit me with the broom. "Oh, Lord. What a mess! Since you think it's so funny, you clean it up!" With a disdainful glance, she flounced across the road and walked home, giggling all the way. The story of the bull in the store was retold many times and got more colorful each time.

———

The time passed with sorting trail cattle from "keepers," branding, and castrating. A mixture of sulphur and turpentine was poured over the cattle when we worked them to kill the ticks.

"How's the tally comin', Aaron?"

"We got two hundred and seven castrated grown bulls, seventy-five good cross-bred steers, and fifty-three barren cows for market."

"Yeah, and some of those old moss backs are old enough to vote!" Pecos was right about that. They were a spotted, speckled and striped collection with heavy long horns. Some horns curved up, a few curved down, some grew nearly straight out, and a few looked like corkscrews. They were thick in the chest and thin in the rump. They weren't much for pretty, but they were free and we aimed to cash in on these cane busters.

We kept all one hundred and three of our cross-bred cows and had added one hundred and twenty-three young longhorn cows and forty-three young heifers to the herd as "keepers." There were several cross-bred and longhorn steers that were too young for the trip, but would be just right for the next one. The cattle gradually settled down, even the Sheriff's "devil" cow. Come spring, we would be ready to go.

4

Sharecroppers and hope

THREE FAMILIES OF FREED Negroes came to the store. A tall middle-aged black man walked to the door and knocked. Mother grabbed a shotgun and cocked both barrels. "What do you want?"

Placing his hands in the air, he began to talk. "Ma'am, we's lookin' fo' work. We ain't hardly et nothin' an de chilren is hungry. We'd work fo' a lil' cornmeal and lard." A ragged child clung to the man's tattered overalls. They looked like starved coachwhip snakes.

Their plight touched her. "Let me get you some food and we'll talk about it. My men folks are close by, so don't start any trouble."

He smiled and nodded his agreement. She pulled out a ten pound sack of cornmeal, a bucket of lard, a five pound bag of dried beans, and a small poke of salt. "Y'all got a skillet to cook with?"

"Yessum, we got all dat. That sho seem like a right smart of food. It mo' dan we need."

"You got more food I don't know about? I see nearly a dozen people counting children. Take it. You can

35

work it out later. Pitch camp here by the store. There's a well and some wood around back."

Logan Morgan wandered over from his shop carrying a shotgun. "Everything alright, Miss Nancy?"

"What is going to happen to these people? They have nowhere to go, nowhere to work, nowhere to live, nothing to eat. I've got empty cabins and fields growing up in weeds. I'm going to see if they'll stay and crop my land on the shares. What's the going rate?"

"If you supply the seed, mule, plow, cabin and groceries, you get half the crop. If you only supply the cabin and land, it is one third."

"These folks don't have anything. I'll offer half shares, but first I'm going to talk to Noah and Aaron."

———————————

"Mother, I guess there isn't anything wrong with it. Do you feel comfortable havin' them here? I'll be gone all summer on the drive to Sedalia."

"I'll be here. I walked through them. I didn't see anybody too scary." Noah advised.

The deal was quickly accepted. They moved into the vacant cabins. Noah assigned parts of fields for them to work. There was old furniture left in the cabins they were glad to get. He brought up three good quality work mules and harness. They would have to share the various farm implements. He distributed seed cotton and corn along with beans, peas, seed potatoes and sweet potatoes and vegetable seed. There were plenty of hand tools in the barn.

"We decided to give each of you a milk cow since you got all those children. Mother gets the first gallon of milk and a dozen eggs a day. The rest is yours. We have hogs that you are to tend and butcher in the winter. Momma gets half the meat and lard. You get the other half, hams, back meat and all. We'll provide the salt. Any time she needs beef, you take care of the butcherin'. She gets half and you get the other half. Momma said she'd provide one pair of shoes a year, and one set of summer clothes, and another for the winter, including the children. If you make things to sell, tobacco, jerky, bacon, extra food or corn, she'll put 'em in the store for ya' and give you half of any cash it brings. I'll tell ya' this; she won't ever cheat ya'.'"

Noah laid off one hundred and twenty acres for them to share. Before dark we could see the mules turning the rich soil and the women weeping and scrubbing. We didn't have a clue if this would work, but it seemed like the thing to do.

———————

That spring, Lipan Apache swept up from Mexico and raided along the San Saba River. It was reported they killed several settlers and drove off thousands of horses and cattle. The Comanche and Kiowa began raiding south of the Red River as far south as the upper Brazos. The Colored Infantry companies and their poorly trained white officers were ill-equipped to fight the world's finest light cavalry.

Outlaws were common in the rough country along the Red River and the Big Thicket of deep East Texas. The triumphant Federal troops dared not show their faces in those areas. Yankees, especially colored Yankees, were favorite targets for lynching. We talked among ourselves how evil days had fallen on Texas. We had seen nothing yet.

———————

Logan Morgan spent days preparing our best wagon for the trip. Every spoke was checked, every rim tightened. Every board was checked for soundness. The wagon was made as waterproof as possible. Every seam was caulked with pitch inside and out. Water barrels and tool boxes were added along the outside. The bows were slotted into place and covered with new heavyweight canvas. An extra tongue, axle, front and rear wheel were fastened under the wagon. Finally, a fresh rawhide skin was soaked, then fastened under the wagon, filled with rocks and allowed to dry. It was where we would carry extra wood and cow chips.

The wagon would be pulled by four well-trained, strong, healthy mules and new harness. This was no time for green-broke animals or broken harness and fittings. The mules we selected were put in a good pasture near the cabin and fed extra corn every day to get them in top shape for the trail.

Shelby, Pecos and I selected four horses each from the herd. We rotated using them to keep their minds on their jobs. We didn't need broncs on the drive. They were kept in the same pasture as the wagon mules and fed added corn.

We had several water-tight kegs and boxes made to fit inside the wagon bed. These would keep things dry in heavy rain or river crossings.

We killed a few cattle to make into jerky and butchered a few hogs that we salted. We bought plenty of coffee and some dried apricots and apples. We had our own corn meal and dried beans. We wouldn't take potatoes. They didn't keep well, and took up too much space and weight.

Our bedrolls were made of heavy waterproof canvas about seven feet square; inside, was a wool blanket and a cotton sheet. It was all folded over on itself, tightly rolled, and held together with leather straps.

There were cast iron pots and pans, blue speckled enameled plates, cups, bowls and utensils plus a huge coffee pot. This was all packed into a special box with a hinged lid to keep out dust and dirt.

"Mamma, what do you think we need to take for doctorin'?"

"A few bars of soap. Cleanin' a wound does a lot of good. Bandages and splints. Probably a bottle of whiskey for disinfecting things and pain. Castor oil to drink for constipation or to rub on sprains. Maybe a bottle of laudanum if somebody gets hurt bad enough to need it, and a bottle of paregoric for diarrhea. Can you think of anythin' else?"

"I learned a little when we worked in the hospital at that Yankee prison camp. I think I could sew somebody up, if it wasn't too bad, and lance a boil or dig out a bullet, maybe. I found some things left at the doctor's office. He died in the war and ain't comin' back, so I borrowed 'em. He had a nice doctor's bag to put everythin' in. There was even a tooth extractor. I sure hope I don't have to use any of this stuff."

A very tall, big, bald-headed man rode up on a dapple gray draft horse and the biggest saddle I had ever seen. He tied his horse and strode up to the porch. "This the Turner place?"

I was resting on the upstairs gallery and told him I'd be right down. "I'm Aaron Turner. Glad to meet ya'. Is there somethin' I can do for ya'?"

"Howdy. Kelly Ray Webb is my name." His wide smile showed an absence of teeth. He was a good six foot seven with a broad framed three hundred pounds. He wasn't slick bald, but nearly so. He wore bib overalls open at the sides and huge brogans big enough to be river barges. "I heared up in Hunt County you was puttin' up a drive to Missouri. I'm the best wagon cook you ever saw. I cooked for our unit durin' the war."

"Where'd you fight?"

"I was at Prairie Grove and Pea Ridge, Arkansas. When my ninety day enlistment was up, I loaded my family and moved to Hunt County near the South Sulphur River. The Ozarks weren't no fit place for families durin' the war. A freighter come through from Waco that knowed a man named Benjamin Tyus. He told me to talk to you."

"Well, we do need a cook. You sure you can do it? And how much pay do you want?"

"I can cook beans, biscuits, steaks, gravy, chili, stew, corn-bread, cobbler and good strong coffee. I'll cook for ya' tonight and breakfast in the mornin'. If it ain't good, I'll go home. If you like it, I want forty dollars a month, no paper money, no bank drafts." Kelly's cooking passed with flying colors. It began a relationship that would span many years.

"Hup cows. Hup." Three drovers were headed west on the Camino Real pushing about fifty head of cattle and a dozen horses. They pushed the stock out on the open prairie south of town. A wide shouldered six foot tall man rode up to the front porch and climbed down. "My name is Michael Dawson. Those boys over there are my sons, Jake, eleven, and Matt, sixteen. We got word you was puttin' together a drive to Missouri. We want to throw some cows in with ya' and hire out the boys as drovers."

"I'm Aaron Turner. I reckon that will work if your boys know what they're doin'."

"Matt can ride anythin' with four legs, and is trained as a farrier. He can rope, drag, tie; you name it, he can do it. Jake is right good with horses. Kind of hoped you could use him as wrangler and cook's helper. He won't need any babysittin'."

"I can speak for Matt, that's my department. I'll let the cook decide about the boy."

Kelly visited with Jake and asked him a few things. He sent him over to a tied mule to see if he could put on a set of hobbles. Jake grabbed the mule by a front foot and quickly slipped on the rawhide hobbles. "You'll do, son."

The Dawsons bedded down by the wagon. After breakfast, we helped them road brand their stock. They were mostly good crossbred steers in good flesh. Matt was a pleasure to watch work a rope. He rarely missed and his stout horse dragged the grown steers to the fire. Jake threw a good heel loop, too. Matt was about five foot ten, and skinny as a rail with blond hair and blue eyes just like Jake. For kids, they were plenty punchy.

———

Sheriff Moore and Logan Morgan had come to Texas together as children and had been like brothers for over forty years. They built their homes close together and had been equal partners in the cattle business for a long time. They had good quality crossbred cattle. They had started their herd with one of my father's Shorthorn bulls bred to native cattle. They had continued to upgrade their cattle over the years until they were as good as could be found east of the Brazos. They hadn't been able to sell much during the war and had a good collection of market ready steers. They added one hundred seventy-three head to our forming herd.

The night before we left there was a big party. Kelly had spent all night roasting a fat steer on a spit over hot oak coals. He had kept it mopped with a secret concoction that smelled delicious. There was a kettle full of pinto beans cooked until they were falling apart tender, seasoned with salt, pepper and bacon fat. There were pans of cornbread served up with bowls of fresh butter along with fruit cobblers. Everyone left in Navasota Crossing was invited, including old Tysoe and our sharecroppers. Matt and Jake made a guitar and fiddle come alive. There was singing and dancing.

A firm hand gripped my shoulder. "Little brother, I don't have much family left, and you're the only brother I got. I ain't got a better friend in the world than you. I'll take care of things here while you're gone, but you make dang sure you come back."

"Noah, I ain't ever been away from you more than a day or two in my whole life. I guess you're stuck with me. I'll be back."

———

"Git up, mules! Move your lazy bones!" Kelly's long whip cracked over the backs of the mules as the wagon lurched forward. The loose horses were started behind the wagon. We pushed five hundred and fifty-nine head of cattle out of the pasture and on to the road. They splashed across the Navasota like a flock of sheep. The road provided a natural trail for the herd to follow. We hadn't gone a quarter of a mile until an old barren longhorn pushed her way to the front. She was white with red spots, a "sabina."

"Looks like we got ourselves a lead cow." Pecos noticed.

"Yeah. They're stayin' together pretty good. I guess runnin' in the same pasture the past few months helped 'em buddy up."

We made about fifteen miles the first day, and reached the banks of the Brazos about half an hour before sunset on the second day. There were the remnants of a once fine two-story house and a neglected small fort. A dilapidated cabin near the river housed the ferryman. A few sharecropper cabins were scattered around what appeared to once have been a prosperous community. We watered the cattle in the river and bedded them down in a meadow of good grass.

As night came on, a mist rose up from the river, adding to the sense of gloom hanging over the bottom land. The cattle seemed restless and unsettled.

"Bad medicine."

"Ah, Pecos, that's just your Injun blood talkin'."

"Maybe. Granny knew things, felt things, that white folks didn't. She said spirits wander in the night where bad things happened."

The screech of an owl made my hair stand up. The cattle were milling around and seemed nervous. A second screech was followed by a deep rumbling as all the cattle got to their feet and began trotting north. The hands in camp heard it, too. They grabbed their night horses and caught up with us in a flash. Pecos was at the left front of the herd and Matt was on the right. Sabina was in the lead, trotting nervously along. "Let 'em run as long as they keep headin' mostly north! If they run for Jericho, we'll try to swing 'em away from the river!" After about a mile, they slowed to a walk. Another mile up the road, a prairie opened up on the right. Sabina saw it, and led the others behind her. They spread out and began to graze. Before too long, they began to bed down. We had been lucky.

Four days passed with quiet travel, good grass and fresh water. On the afternoon of May 30, we reached Captain Tyus' ranch. He had sent riders ahead to let down the fence and help us turn the cattle in on the lush grass.

———————————

"Aaron, it's good to see you! There's Pecos, too. You got a nice set of cattle put together. Have you had any trouble?"

"Not much. It's sure good to see you, sir. How many head have you got for the drive?"

"I've got three hundred and thirteen head of stags and barren cows, mostly longhorns. My neighbors have thrown in some, too. The Carters sent over fifty-one head of nice crossbred steers. Their boys volunteered for the drive. The older, Levi, is about fourteen. Luke is about a year or two younger. They're good, tough kids. They'll do a good job for you. The Shepard family sent thirty-seven head of gentle home raised longhorn steers. They're good and fat. Their boy, Kyle, is going, too. He's about fourteen, but a good hand. All the boys brought some decent range ponies with them. They aren't as big as the horses you raise, but I think they'll get them to Missouri and back. Did you get your pay issues figured out?"

"Yessir. All the drovers get thirty dollars a month and found, going and comin' home. Kelly, the cook, draws forty. Pecos is segundo, so he gets thirty-five dollars and I'll draw out an even fifty as trail boss. Every head of live cattle at the start of the drive counts as one share of whatever we get in Sedalia, after expenses."

"That's exactly what we talked about earlier. That's fair to everyone. Can you boss 'em?

"The trail hands? We got that worked out with our bunch and I don't think these new boys will be any trouble."

"You are the oldest sixteen year old I ever saw. Sixteen going on twenty-six."

"Cap, you know how much war ages a man. I sure don't feel sixteen. Pecos is the only one that knows how old I am anyway. This trip ain't gonna be easy, but after what I went through in the war, I know I can get it done."

5

The long trail before us

THE WAGON ROAD TO DALLAS
was rutted and dusty. The one thousand and sixty head
submitted to the leadership of "Ol' Sabina" as if she had
been elected to the job. Dust hovered over us in a cloud you
could see, smell and taste. The road was fenced on both
sides much of the way which made driving them easy. The
hundred miles to Dallas would give me a chance to know
the rest of the crew. I knew Pecos like the back of my hand
and he was the closest person to me except my brother,
Noah. He had my back any time, any day, and I trusted
him without question. Shelby was a different matter. I had
known him for six months. There was a lot to like about
him. He knew his job, was good at doing it and not afraid
to work. He was hard as nails. But there was a different
twist to him that went all the way to the bone.

Matt Dawson could handle a horse as well as any
hand on the drive. He worked as a farrier, just like Pecos,
and could stay up with him shoe for shoe. Those two
became fast friends. He was easy going, and had a quick
dry wit. Pecos summed Matt up pretty well: "That boy's

made of rawhide. He'll do to ride the river any day." From Pecos, that was a big compliment.

Kelly had latched onto Jake like one of his own kids. "I got a boy named Jake at home. Reminds me a lot of that boy." He taught him everything he could about camp cooking and was always patient with him. Jake always seemed to bust his hump to keep Kelly happy. He did a real good job with the remuda. He was a born natural with horses. I never heard him complain once. He put in days that would make a grown man tired. Matt kept an eye out for his little brother. Jake made sure he earned Matt's approval, which he generously granted.

I found myself drawn to Kelly. He was much older than the rest of us. I was guessing he was close to fifty, but you couldn't tell it the way that big man worked. He liked to talk about anything, but if a fellow listened, Kelly usually had something worth listening to. Pecos claimed Kelly's jaws must be double jointed. I liked to hear him talk about his family, and I discovered that he was wise in his own ways. He was a good judge of character. I talked with him about the crew sometimes.

"What do you think of the Shepard kid? I kinda like him."

"Well, for starters, he ain't much younger than you, trail boss. He's a good kid and tries hard. He just needs a little experience."

"What about Luke and Levi?"

"They're good boys. That older one talks nearly as much as me. I like the little one, too. He's a little quiet, but both of 'em got plenty of try. They'll be alright."

"You see any trouble spots?"

"That ain't my place to say, but since you asked me, I'll tell you what I think. Shelby worries me. He's got a short fuse and a chip on his shoulder. But there's something else."

"You gonna keep it a secret?"

"I'll tell it to ya. I know I seen that boy at Prairie Grove. His unit camped next to us."

"He said something about being there, then being on detached duty."

"Shelby rode with Quantrill. Quantrill was supposed to be

a Confederate captain; some say the government revoked his commission. His lieutenant was "Bloody Bill" Anderson. Jesse and Frank James rode with Quantrill, just like the Daltons and Coulters. You know what happened at Lawrence, Kansas?"

"Yeah, I do."

"All them old men, boys, cripples and women shot down like dogs and the town burned. It wasn't no kinda war. It was murder. Fort Baxter was even worse. It ain't a day's ride from Lawrence. Some of them colored soldiers got caught out of their fort. Quantrill had 'em way outnumbered. Had 'em surrender and throw down their guns. Then they shot those four hundred unarmed colored boys dead in the Fort Smith road. They went raidin' on down into Texas. They robbed the Preston store, then rode into Denison and Gainesville and shot or hung anybody who had ever had any Union leanin's. The Confederates finally had to send a Brigade of cavalry under Kirby Smith to run 'em out of Texas. They caused so much trouble up in Arkansas, that's why we moved to Texas."

"It could be a long ride to Sedalia."

———————

Dallas wasn't much to see at the time, but there was a hint of greater things to come. It sat on the Trinity River. Steamboats could come up all the way from the Gulf. The main east-west road across north Texas ran through Dallas, as did the major north-south road from Oklahoma deep into the heart of Texas. There was already talk of a railroad into Dallas. Shelby and Pecos rode into Dallas to partake of some of its "coarser pleasures."

At Dallas we picked up Preston Trail, the wagon road north to the Red River. It ran just west of some higher ground called Preston Ridge. Preston sat just above the flood zone of the Red River. We stopped at the trading post there. We didn't need much except some more tobacco for Kelly. He chewed it like a beaver eating willow trees.

Red Bluff was a natural narrowing of the rocky bluffs. It worked as a natural funnel to push cattle into the water. The Red River was notorious for quicksand and flash floods. Here it had a hard bottom and the Oklahoma bank had a slow gentle slope of rocky soil that made it easier for the cattle to get out.

Pecos rode the ford and found it was solid. The river was down enough that Kelly was able to walk the mules across. Sabina pushed right into the muddy red water and the other cattle followed like the children of Israel following Moses.

We made a few miles north of the river where there was good grazing and fresh clean water. Jake fetched plenty of wood for cooking, then rode herd on the remuda to let them graze before picketing them for the night. Since we were now in Indian Territory, he used hobbles as an extra level of precaution against theft. Kelly cooked the usual beans and bacon, but had bought a small sack of flour to make biscuits and gravy. It was the first biscuits we had eaten since starting the drive.

———

The next morning, I rode ahead of the herd a couple of miles. I spotted a small band of Indians. They stopped with their rifles and bows above their heads in a sign of peace. We rode toward each other until we were only a few yards apart. They showed no hostile intent. Pecos, on the left point, had seen them and came loping up. They were dressed in a variety of clothes from beaded buckskins to plaid cotton shirts. One older Indian had an air of authority. He spoke first in words and signs I sure didn't know.

"He says they are Shawnee and this is their land. We are welcome to the grass and water, but we can't settle here. They collect a toll for passage."

"Captain Tyus said to expect this at some places. He sent some silver dollars with me to pay the tolls. Tell 'em we got just over one thousand head. See how twenty silver dollars strikes 'em."

He and Pecos parlayed with their hands. "He says that is good. I think you coulda got it cheaper. He is gonna give you somethin' so other Shawnee won't try to make you pay again. Keep it to use when we come back through. They got a fresh killed doe they wanna give us. You know that means we gotta give them somethin'."

"Take the deer back to the wagon. Tell Kelly I gotta buy three pouches from him. I'll double what he paid."

Pecos was back fast with the tobacco. "Ol' Biscuit sure is cussin' you, but I got the tobacco."

I handed the tobacco to the leader. He gave me a beaded leather strap that was our ticket through Shawnee lands.

Through the humid summer days we slowly pushed the herd ten or twelve miles a day, letting them graze and fatten on the good grass as they ambled along. We had settled into a routine. After breakfast at daybreak, Kelly drove the wagon ahead of the herd, with Jake moving the horses a hundred yards back, letting them take their time. "Old Sabina" wasn't far behind, always at the front of the herd, holding her place with hooves and horns. Whenever she got to her feet, the other cattle started to get up, stretch and scratch, and slowly assume their places in the herd. I would ride ahead until I found a place to bed the herd for the night. Pecos at left point was in charge, and he set the pace for the day. Shelby was stationed at right point, with Kyle on the right flank, and Matt on the left. As the least experienced, Luke and Levi were assigned to ride drag. We carried jerky, corn pones and leftover bacon to snack on during the day. There was no lunch break north of the Red River. Lukewarm water from the canteens was all we had to drink.

The Carter boys had brought their hunting rifles. When there was time, they would slip off after supper into the brush. They brought back sacks of squirrels, a few turkeys, and several deer. They were dead shots.

Kelly's cooking was more than adequate. He treated us to squirrel stew, fried turkey, chicken fried venison, biscuits and gravy, chili, pinto beans, and cornbread, either baked or fried. Breakfast was always cornbread, thickly sliced salt pork fried crisp, and lots of strong black coffee. Once in a while he would treat us to a cobbler made with dried apples or apricots. One evening, Jake found a thicket of wild plums. Kelly made a big cobbler that was kind of tart. Pecos made a sour face. "That cobbler coulda been real good if he weren't so stingy with the sugar. I bet he counts every grain of sugar in the whole thing."

Not every day was routine. One evening, while Shelby and I were on night herd together, he rode over near my horse. "We gotta talk. I got a boil comin' up on my butt big as a turnip. Kelly gave me some salt pork to draw it to a head. It's pointin' now ready to cut."

"Why you tellin' me?"

"I know you got that medical kit, and Pecos said you learned a little doctorin' durin' the war."

"Yeah, mighty little. I'll try to lance it when we get off shift."

Pecos and Matt rode out to meet us for their watch. We rode on into camp. I woke Kelly up. "I need that medical bag out of the wagon and a bottle of bug juice."

Kelly grinned. "Ol' Sour Puss decided that boil is ready to blow?"

"Yeah. Let's get it done."

We gave Shelby a pan of hot water and lye soap and told him to wash himself off real well. When he was done, he leaned against the side of the wagon with the flap of his cotton drawers down.

"Woo wee! I seen towns smaller than that sucker! Better watch out, looks like she's ready to blow!"

"Biscuit, would you just shut up. This is bad enough without you yappin'!"

I took a clean rag and wiped the area with whiskey, and fished a scalpel out of the doctor's bag. "Kelly, that sure looks bad. Maybe we oughta use a butcher knife." We shared a pull on the whiskey bottle while it was open.

"Ain't you gonna give me some of that stuff?"

"Naw, I figure you're gonna pass out and not feel anythin' anyway."

Shelby reached to hitch up his drawers, but Kelly grabbed him by the wrist. "We just got your rear end clean. Son, if we don't lance that you're gonna git real sick. We're just rawhidin' ya. But it needs doin' now. We'll share the scamper juice after it's done."

"Grab that board tight, Shelby. It's gonna hurt some."

I made a cut into the bulging head of the angry boil. I'll be darn if it didn't blow foul gray pus back on Kelly and me both. Shelby let out such a howl, the youngsters came to watch.

"Ain't you done yet?"

"Nope. I gotta squeeze out the rest of that pus. It's gonna hurt." I pushed from each angle toward the lanced opening. Pus and black blood rolled out like a nasty mudslide. Kelly kept it wiped up with a clean rag so I could see. Finally nothing but red blood came out. "I guess that's it. Have a few swallows of this." He sucked on that whiskey bottle like a nursing colt.

Levi couldn't miss an opportunity to pop off. "I seen smaller hogs than that thing!"

"Aw, shut up you snot-nosed Yankee lover."

Kiowa! A dozen warriors rode our direction. I waved for Pecos who came galloping up.
They didn't hold their bows and rifles in the sign of peace. I was a little worried.

"Wohaw!" One demanded. "Wohaw!" He raised his hand with his fingers spread.

"They want five steers!"

"The hell I will! You tell him one steer or eleven silver dollars." Pecos translated.

"Wohaw!" He raised three fingers. About that time from the hills above the trail, another twenty to thirty Kiowa appeared.

"Aaron, there ain't enough of us to fight 'em. Looks like the price is three head. That's only nine buck back in Texas. It shore ain't worth gettin' killed over."

"Alright. Have the boys cut out the two sorriest steers in the bunch and the Sheriff's ol' devil cow branded TM 45. I hope they choke on her."

The spokesman smiled to one of the braves who was carrying an ornate short war lance. The brave took off at a gallop heading for the wagon and Kelly. He circled the wagon at full speed then reined his horse to an abrupt stop next to the wagon seat. He handed Kelly the lance and sped away. Pecos said it was our safe passage through their land. The Kiowa trotted the three head of sorry, stringy beef into the timber along the trail and disappeared.

We didn't have any more Indian troubles. We finally reached the valley of the Arkansas River. The valley was broad and lush. We threw the cattle out to graze in the thick grass and set up camp in the hills south of the river. The trail lay just below the confluence of the north and south forks of the Arkansas. The water was green, deep and about a quarter mile wide. Pecos rode up. "It don't look much like the same river we were on at Fort Hindman. I sure don't miss that place."

"No. It's a lot of river down there, but bet this will be all we want and then some. At least there ain't no damn Yankee ironclads shootin' at us."

My thoughts drifted away to those days from the end of 1862 until the fort fell and we were captured in January of '63. Noah, Pinckney and David were all with me then. I missed all of them. David was the closest person to a father I ever knew and Noah wasn't just my brother, but my best friend in the world. Only three and a half years had passed, but it seemed like a lifetime. My world, our world, had been turned upside down and ripped apart by the war. Nothing would ever be the same again. But, I was a Turner and a third generation Texan. I came from pretty sturdy stock. I knew whatever happened, we'd find our way.

"You still with us, boss? Seems like we lost you there for a minute."

"Sorry. I was thinkin' about how much the war took from us and how much everythin' has changed."

"Yeah, I know. I ain't got a livin' soul left in my family. I'm stuck with you for kinfolks. How sorry can it get?" Pecos grinned at me.

We checked the river crossing. There was a deep narrow channel near the south bank, then a wide sandbar in the middle of the river. North of the sandbar was a wide deep channel with a strong current.

When we emerged on the north bank, we found we had drifted over a hundred yards downstream.

"We're gonna have to start the wagon and livestock across upstream a ways so they'll come out here where there is an easy bank to climb. I'm a little worried they may bunch up on the sandbar, so we'll have to make sure the boys keep them moving."

We knew the mules couldn't swim the wagon across the big channel. It was too deep, too wide and the current was too strong. Kelly had a good idea. "Unhitch my mules on the sand bar and swim 'em across harnessed. We'll let them drag over a couple of heavy ropes, one for them to pull the wagon across and one to tie to the back of the wagon on the upstream side. A couple of men on horseback could keep the rear of the wagon from swingin' downstream." We agreed.

Levi and Luke had taken their hunting rifles up river and had come back with a big fat doe. Kelly pulled out some flour he had been saving and made biscuits and gravy to go with the fried venison. He topped that off with a dried apricot cobbler. Matt and Jake got down their guitar and fiddle and entertained us after supper until they were too tired to play anymore. It was one of those nights we would remember and talk about.

_____

The hands took off their hats, boots, and clothes and put them in the wagon along with their saddles. They would face the river bareback and in their summer short drawers. Kelly and Jake drove the mules into the Arkansas. It was only a few yards until the big bay mules were swimming hard across the current of the narrow channel. The lead mules quickly found some bottom on the edge of the sandbar and rose up out of the water pulling hard, followed by the wheel mules. They drove to the edge of the sandbar and unhitched the mules from the wagon. Jake dropped their trace chains and unhitched them from one another so they could swim freely. He and Kelly fastened a rope to the hames of two of the mules and held on as they directed the mules into the deep channel. The strong mules handled the crossing like champions. Once they were across, Jake hooked the four mules together again and fastened them to the rope leading to the wagon tongue. Kelly looped the other rope around the smooth trunk of a cottonwood tree. It had been fasten to the upstream corner of the back of the wagon. Kyle and Matt swam their horses over and tied on to the second rope. At Kelly's signal, Jake slapped the drive lines across the wet backs of the mules.

"Hup mules!" They pulled against the heavy rope until it drew tight. The wagon started to ease forward into the deep channel. The current immediately started moving the wagon downstream. Kyle and Matt eased their horses forward until the rope on the rear of the wagon was tight. If the back started to swing farther downstream than the front, they eased their horses forward until the wagon was straight again. Soon the wagon was on the sloping bank, dripping water, but safe and dry on the inside. The mules were hitched directly to the tongue and the wagon driven up the slope and down the trail to that night's campground.

Kyle and Matt swam their horses back across the river and started the remuda across. They stopped at the sandbar to consider the deep channel, but stepped right in and swam to the north bank. Old Sabina saw the horses leaving and she instinctively followed them to the river's edge. The other cattle came right along behind her. They swam the first channel and stopped on the sandbar. Seeing Sabina hesitate, Matt eased up to her and slapped her on the rump with his rope. Not one to be hurried, she gave Matt the "evil eye," pondered the deep water momentarily, and then stepped into the channel as if the whole thing was her idea. The others crowded dutifully into the swirling green water.

Luke and Levi came behind pushing the last few reluctant head off the sandbar. As the first cattle climbed out of the water on the north bank the boys put their horses into the strong deep current, holding on to their horses' tails. A rain storm somewhere upstream had caused a huge cottonwood tree in full leaf to topple into the river. Kyle saw it and yelled a warning. "Levi! Luke! Look upstream! A big tree's comin'!"

Levi looked up in time to see the danger and swam out of the path of the huge tree. His horse was scraped across the rump by the branches, but not hurt. Luke stayed with his horse. The current swept the tree down upon them. The leafy top of the tree squarely hit Luke and his horse and forced them to the bottom of the deep channel. In seconds, the panicked horse bobbed to the surface squealing in fear and thrashing the water desperately as it swam for the bank. Luke was nowhere to be seen. Suddenly, his head poked through the churning water a hundred feet downstream. He was struggling and obviously in trouble.

Shelby sunk his bare heels into his horse's dripping flanks and galloped along the edge of the river until he was fifteen or twenty feet ahead of Luke. He charged his horse straight into the deep channel and let him swim to the middle. He bailed off and swam to Luke just before the current carried him away. Matt rode down and threw a long rope to Shelby. Holding Luke under one arm, he held on to the rope and let Matt tow them in.

Luke was in a bad way; his color was gray and he was barely breathing. I rolled him on his stomach and pushed hard on his back to shove some of the water out of him. I turned him face up and gave a hard push on his distended belly. River water spewed everywhere. He coughed and gasped, then vomited up more water. He was shaking and coughing, but he was alive.

Kelly brought blankets for Luke and Shelby. Levi knelt beside his brother crying quietly. Luke's eyes fluttered open. "Am I dead?"

"No, you ain't." Levi sniffed.

"I seen angels and stuff I never seen before. It was real pretty. Hey, would somebody catch my horse? If I ain't dead, I'm gonna need him."

We all laughed, more from relief than anything else. Kyle had already caught his horse. Matt carried him to the wagon and they cleared a place for him to rest.

Kelly caught me by the elbow. "That boy swallowed half the Arkansas. I think he oughta rest a couple of days so he don't get pneumonia."

I nodded agreement. We settled into dry clothes and got comfortable in camp. We got Luke properly dried off and bedded down. Kelly fixed him some strong black coffee with a generous helping of bug juice. Not being used to ardent spirits, Luke was snoring in his bed in twenty minutes.

Levi tentatively approached Shelby. "Thanks for what you done for my brother." He reached out his hand to Shelby who ignored it.

"I'd a done the same thing for one of them colored Yankee soldiers."

"I reckon you might, but this was my brother. Thank you, Shelby."

Shelby's face colored. "Oh the hell with it. You're welcome. It was a fool thing for me to do anyway. I'm glad the little rat's gonna be alright. He's a pretty good kid for a snot-nosed Yankee lovin' brat." He shook Levi's hand and walked away.

———

Two days and nights of rest on the rolling prairie north of the Arkansas River had been just what all of us had needed. The long days, summer heat, and humidity had drained us and we were ready for a break. Luke looked better and stronger by the day, but his near drowning had sure taken the starch out of him. He still coughed up a little river water, but hadn't had any fever and looked generally better. Several of the boys had made cane poles. Kelly had some line and hooks, and was kind enough to provide bacon rind for bait. The catfish they brought in were a welcome change from bacon and beans. Levi had stayed by Luke the first day. But when he was convinced he wasn't going to die, he took his rifle and returned with two tom turkeys.

"We try not to shoot the hen turkeys, especially in the summer when they's tendin' little 'uns, but these here toms ain't got nothin' to do." They were quite tasty fried.

The morning we pulled out, I was scouted a couple of miles ahead of the herd. I met a lone rider in a large black hat on an ancient small gray mule. I reined over to the side of the trail to wait for him.

"Howdy, white man. You got any tobaccy?" He had long gray hair pulled back in tight braids. He was thin as a reed. He wore a beautifully beaded buckskin vest under a lightweight gray coat, old greasy buckskin leggings, and plain moccasins. The mule looked as old as Methuselah. "My name is John Walking Bear. I'm the trail fee collector for the Cherokee Nation."

I pushed my horse down close enough I could shake his brown boney hand. "My name is Aaron Turner. I'm the trail boss for this herd. We got one thousand fifty-seven cattle, and I ain't got any tobaccy on me, but there is some in the wagon."

"I've been watchin' you since you crossed the river. You been in the Cherokee Strip since then. We charge a silver dollar a hundred head, and it's free comin' back. We don't need any wohaw; we got plenty of our own."

"I been expectin' someone to show up. You're the friendliest one yet. Them Kiowa was none too friendly. Would eleven dollars even work for you?"

"I reckon that would work fine. Here's a receipt to show you paid. You headin' to Sedalia?"

"That's the plan. How's the grass up that way?"

"There's been good rain; the grass is thick and green. Keep followin' the Neosho River as far as you can. You'll have plenty of good water and grass for a long ways. Some of them farmers in Missouri ain't too friendly to Texas herds. They think the Texas cattle make theirs sick and die. Me, I don't care."

Kelly came along with the wagon. Jake was right behind him with the remuda. "This is John Walking Bear, Cherokee agent. This big fella here is Kelly, the best trail cook north of the Red River. The young 'un is Jake, the wrangler and cook's helper. Kelly, it seems our friend is out of tobacco. Could I buy another three bags from you for a dollar?"

"Nice to meet ya, Chief. Yeah, I got plenty of tobaccy. You ever know me to run out?"

"Care if I climb up in the wagon with you awhile to let my old mule rest for a spell? We're both pretty old and wore out."

"Come on up. We'll swap some lies about what rascals we was when we was young. You think that ol' mule can make it another mile?"

"He's already lasted longer than your hair and teeth, white man." We had a good laugh at Kelly's expense.

"We better get movin'; Ol' Sabina is about to catch us."

———————

The Neosho was lined with groves of cottonwood trees and oaks. The water was clean and clear. There was abundant pasture everywhere. Kelly fixed his usual supper of bacon, beans and cornbread. Old John Walking Bear ate like a starving man and drank enough coffee to float a river boat. "You boys are Rebs ain't ya'?"

"Me and Pecos and Kelly are."

"My people fought with the south, too. Chief Stand Waitie commanded the Cherokee Rifles. He keeps the peace around here now, too."

"We fought with the Cherokee Rifles at Resaca. They were plenty tough."

"Plenty Cherokee boys didn't come home." He filled his pipe and puffed thoughtfully for a minute, then looked into the night sky and blew smoke at the half moon, the earth and the four winds. He then passed the pipe to Kelly, Pecos and me. We repeated his process, which was a form of prayer of thanks to the Creator. Shelby walked away shaking his head. The old man then rolled up in a thin blanket and slept snoring by the fire.

Old John rode along with us all the way to Baxter Springs, Kansas, right on the Oklahoma line. He seemed to enjoy the company and the food. The youngsters really warmed up to him. There was a ruin of an earthen fort at Baxter Springs next to a tidy trading post and prosperous farm. John stopped abruptly. "This is a place of wandering spirits. Many black soldiers were murdered here by Quantrill's raiders. Don't camp here. It's bad medicine. I'll look for you on your way back."

I rode in to the trading post to pick up some flour, salt and tobacco. There were fresh onions, squash, green beans and sweet corn for sale. I bought enough for a couple of meals. I bought a sack of fresh peaches and a small sack of sugar. We would eat well the next few days.

There was still a faint odor of death about the place, especially near the collapsed burial trenches. Here and there bone protruded from the cursed ground. John was right. There was bad medicine here. We rode on a few miles farther up the Neosho to bed the cattle. Pecos rode up beside me. "You seen Shelby all day? He talked Matt into taking right point."

I found no tracks this side of the Neosho. I crossed over and backtracked down the opposite bank. Shelby had been riding a blue roan horse that morning. I saw it near the river. I eased my horse into a trot. "Shelby, its Aaron. I'm coming in." There was no answer so I eased on in. I saw Shelby sitting on a log near the river with a pistol in his hand.

"I didn't ask for no company."

"I came to find my right point rider."

"I quit. I ain't goin' no farther."

"You signed up for a job. We don't have anyone that can take your place without leaving us shorthanded. I never thought a good Reb like you would leave us high and dry."

"I ain't a good Reb; never was. I rode with Quantrill. I was at Lawrence and Baxter Springs. What we did there was cold-blooded murder. Do you even know who I am? General Joe Shelby is my brother. He's a hero; I'm an outlaw."

"Lots of us had to do plenty of things we didn't like in the war. It was especially bad up in Kansas, Missouri and the Ozarks."

"You don't understand. It was war at Prairie Grove and Pea Ridge, but it was killin' for the taste of blood at Lawrence and Baxter Springs. My own brother disowned me."

"Ain't a one of us tried to pass judgment on you. We judge a man on how he does his work and treats folks. You've done your work as good as anybody. You saved Pecos from that rattler and pulled Luke out of the river. As far as we're concerned, you're one of us."

He just stared at me. "I'm wanted in Kansas, Missouri and Texas. What am I supposed to do?" He eased the hammer of his pistol down to half-cock and spun the cylinder.

"We all got our own demons. I got mine only Noah knows about. I deal with them every day. I'm only sixteen; I got my whole life ahead of me."

"I'm twenty. Maybe if the law don't catch up to me for a while, I can get past all this. He slipped his pistol back in the holster and stood up. I guess you still got a drover, if you'll have me."

———

Our third day in Missouri, a county sheriff and a band of armed farmers trotted up to me ahead of the herd. "Mister, you and them Texas cattle ain't welcome here."

"Sheriff, there's some folks in Sedalia mighty anxious to get these cattle. My name's Turner, Aaron Turner." I rode up to the sheriff and offered my hand.

He seemed surprised at my approach. "Wilber Ellis. Them Texas cattle make our local stock sick. There's a quarantine."

"Yeah. I understand why these folks are worried. I heard the Texas Fever is caused by ticks. Is that right?" The farmers nodded in agreement. "Before we left Texas we drenched the cattle with turpentine and sulphur. The ticks fell off dead in half an hour." The farmers exchanged glances. The Sheriff looked unconvinced. "Come on. Ride through 'em. You'll see they're healthy and not eat up with ticks."

Pecos and Shelby held up the herd while our unexpected visitors rode through the cattle. "Now, Sheriff, ain't that the cleanest lookin' herd you ever saw. Tell ya what I'd like to do. You men pick us out places ten or twelve miles apart that have grass and water, but no local cattle near the place. We'll keep our stock from mixin' with yours all the way to Sedalia. I'll pay ten Yankee silver dollars to the man that owns the pasture and ten to the man that makes the deal."

The farmers nodded in agreement. The sheriff spoke up. "I ain't got authority out of this county, but I'll see what I can do. I'll get back to ya. If anybody up the line gives ya trouble, have 'em telegraph me."

The sheriff did a good job. There was green grass and clean water at each stop, and no cattle closer than a mile from our herd. He was pretty good company and helped with the cattle. The Missouri landscape was dotted with prosperous, pretty farms. I liked it, but it wasn't Texas.

6

Trading Texas steers for Yankee dollars

BANNERS PROCLAIMED "Welcome Texas Drovers!" Flags and bunting fluttered everywhere. Cattle buyers greeted us with cigars and bids for the cattle. We had arrived with one thousand fifty-eight mature, grass fattened slaughter ready animals. The buyers had been expecting just longhorns, but half the herd was good crossbred stock. These were healthy and heavy. We were the first herd up from Texas that summer, and the north was craving beef. Some offered thirty dollars a head. A few even offered forty dollars for the crossbreds. The best offer we got was thirty-five dollars a head straight across from a cattle buyer named Joseph McCoy from Chicago. We shook hands on the deal and drove the cattle to the shipping pens at the railroad.

The cattle were counted again as they moved into the wooden pens, confirming our count. "Well, Aaron, they're our responsibility now. Walk down to the bank with me and we'll settle up."

Kyle, Jake, Matt, Levi and Luke walked along with

Pecos and me to the bank. "Every one of y'all is totin' some kinda gun."

"We don't aim to let nobody rob us after all that work." Levi popped off. "Besides, you and Pecos is both packin' iron." I had to laugh at the little army of teenagers descending on the bank. Woe be to the man who got in their way! Then I noticed Shelby was nowhere to be found. Then I remembered he was wanted in Missouri.

My motley-looking posse sat in the bank lobby as I met with Mr. McCoy and the banker. "Alright, Mr. Turner, that's one thousand fifty-eight head at thirty-five dollars a head. That comes to thirty-seven thousand and thirty dollars. That's a large sum of money. We'll discuss how you want to take it out."

"Aaron, I'm gonna leave you here with Banker Glenn. Don't let him give you any wooden nickels. I hope you'll consider having a large part of the money wire transferred to Texas. It's safe and beats getting robbed. I made arrangements for you and your drovers to go to Chin Li's Chinese laundry and bathhouse as my treat, and I have prepaid for your meal at Delmonico's Restaurant. It is the best in Sedalia. I appreciate your business very much."

"You didn't have to do all that, but we do appreciate it, too. You gave us a fair price for the cattle."

"They're exactly what I wanted, even better. I want to do business with you again in the future. A man of your age to have accomplished what you did has a bright future."

Strange shrill voices in a language I didn't understand floated out of the back of the shop. Steam rose over curtained walls. There was a strong, clean smell of lye soap in the humid air. I rang a bell and a man I thought to be Chin Li came to the front in an exotic robe and strange hat.

"My name's Turner."

"Oh, yes. Mistah Turner. Mistah McCoy said to expect you. You get deluxe treatment. Bath, shave, haircut, laundry. All paid for. All your men. Come, come." This was followed by hand clapping and shouted orders in what I took for Chinese. We were directed into an area of his establishment that had row after row of galvanized bath tubs separated by curtained partitions. We were instructed to hand out our dirty clothes, hats and boots through the curtains to waiting workers. I was naked as a jaybird, but I was keeping my gun with me. We were handed wash cloths, towels and bars of lye soap. I settled into the tub of very warm water and began to wash off a summer's worth of trail dust. I was startled by a woman's voice behind me. Although the water was already pretty soapy, I quickly covered up the part that mattered most with a washcloth.

"You get shave now." The older Chinese woman washed my face with a hot soapy rag, and then lathered it with a brush and cup. She produced a very wicked looking straight razor. "You hold bery still." She deftly gave me the best shave I had ever had and wrapped my face with a hot towel. I was just about to start to relax when another voice spoke from behind me.

"Cut hair now." The washcloth quickly returned to its strategic location as the elderly Chinese woman quickly cut my shaggy red hair. She then poured a pitcher of warm water over my head and began to scrub my hair, followed by another pitcher of water. She was gone as quickly as she had appeared. I soaked and relaxed in the warm water for a good while. A hand reached through the curtain and my freshly laundered and ironed clothes on the floor were set on the floor. My hat had been brushed, starched, steamed and reshaped until it looked a lot better. My freshly cleaned and polished boots appeared next. I climbed out and dried off. The cleaned, starched and ironed clothes felt strange, but looked pretty good with the hat and boots. As we reassembled in the lobby, Chin Li passed around a bottle of Bay Rum to splash on our faces and a handful of peppermints.

Jake, Kyle, Luke and Levi didn't have a whisker between the four of them, but they had proudly accepted their shaves, and generously splashed on the Bay Rum. "Oh, Mistah Turner. Everybody look bery nice! Come back again, please."

"Gentlemen, welcome to Delmonico's Restaurant. Mr. McCoy

has taken care of the cost of your meal and reserved you a table. I'll be bringing your meal out; I hope you enjoy it."

He returned with a large tray of oysters on the half-shell on a bed of ice. "These arrived packed in a barrel of ice this morning. Just use the small fork, pull the oyster out of the shell and eat it. They're delicious!"

Not wanting to appear uneducated, I grabbed one from the tray, speared the slimy gray glob from the shell and popped it in my mouth. I quickly spit it into my hand and threw it in the spittoon. "Whew, that tastes like snake guts!" They all had a good laugh at my expense.

Pecos decided to show off and tried to eat one. Three chews and it came up on the table. "Ugh! Fish bait!"

Luke and the others finally goaded Levi enough that he tried an oyster. He managed to chew it up and swallow it, but it all came back up in his brother's hat. At this point, we were laughing enough to draw a little attention.

"I'm sorry the oysters were not to your taste." The waiter sniffed. He quickly removed them from the table and returned with a basket of rolls. Those rolls disappeared as quick as he brought them out, followed by three more baskets. "That's even better than my corn-bread." Kelly claimed.

The waiter in the fancy clothes came back with a huge tray covered with plates. Each plate held a thick juicy steak hanging over the edges of the plate. "Them steaks are as big as my hat!" Jake grinned. They were from corn-fed beef and tender as butter. Large bowls of fresh green beans cooked with bacon were set out on the table, along with huge bowls piled high with fluffy mashed potatoes beside a boat-load of brown gravy. As plates and bowls emptied, others took their places. As we started to slow down, the waiter came back with a tray of real three-layered chocolate cake.

"Would you gentlemen like coffee with your cake?" He brought around a big coffee pot and started filling cups, but the first ones were empty before he made his way around the table. "Mr. McCoy said you would like your coffee extra strong. You seem to be enjoying it." He kept bringing more coffee until we couldn't drink anymore.

We finally got up to leave, so full we could hardly waddle to the door. Jake stopped to shake hands with the waiter. "Mister, you done real good on everythin' except them ersters."

———

The next morning, we were at the bank when it opened. I had figured each man's wages. We had spent three months on the trail and would be a month and a half getting home. Each of the drovers took his pay in silver dollars and gold coins. Jake couldn't hold his pants up from all the weight in his pockets. After paying the hands and subtracting out my pay and expenses, there was over thirty-five thousand dollars to be divided among the various owners, depending on the number of head they provided for the drive. Captain Tyus had requested his share be wire transferred to his bank account in Waco. I watched as Mr. Glenn wrote a note to a clerk who soon returned with a telegram and a receipt for a deposit of over ten thousand dollars to the Captain's account. I was somewhat leery of this type of transaction. I had more than enough experience with worthless pieces of paper from the Confederacy.

Mr. Glenn looked at me thoughtfully. "Well, Aaron, how do you want your money?"

"My part is better than eleven thousand dollars, but I gotta split that with Momma, Noah and Pecos. How about a thousand dollar bank draft and ten thousand in gold?"

The banker looked like he had swallowed his chewing tobacco. "It will take weeks to get that much gold in here. I could give you five thousand in gold and a bank draft for six thousand. It would be honored at any bank in Texas.

"Good in paper or coin?"

"I'll be honest with you, it's more likely to be paper money than coin. Hard money is scarce."

"So is good Texas beef. We got boxes of worthless paper money at home."

"I understand. If you want to wait, I'll get all of it here in gold or silver. I don't know how you'll get home with all of it. You could get robbed or lose it crossing a river."

"Well, I don't know."

"I tell you what. I'll telegraph the Cattleman's Bank in Waco where Captain Tyus does his business. We'll open you an account and wire the money to them. I'll tell them you want to withdraw part of it in coin when you get there."

"You got a deal. But I'm taking the five thousand in coin with me."

The Dawsons, Shepards and Carters had all wanted their money wired to Waco, as did Sheriff Moore and Logan Morgan. Maybe they trusted banks more than I did. The correct amounts were divided out, and invisible dollars were sent by telegram to a bank I had never seen.

We hit the stores in Sedalia. I found a pretty blue dress for Mother and a doll for Alice. I bought a striped shirt for Noah and one for me. Most of the drovers bought shirts or pants. Luke Carter walked up to the counter with a shirt, a pair of pants and a doll.

"Is that doll for you, son?" The storekeeper laughed.

Luke pointed straight at Levi. "Nah. It's for him, but he's too shy to buy it."

Kelly restocked the wagon with lots of good stuff and plenty of flour. He said we had enough money that we didn't have to eat corn-bread every day. Matt and Pecos threw new shoes on all the horses and mules. We were about ready to head back to Texas.

7

Bringing home the bacon

THE MULES WERE FRESH AND rested. The newly oiled leather harness creaked with every step and the trace chains jangled as they trotted down the Shawnee Trail. They seemed to sense we were heading home to Texas. We made thirty miles the first day. The Missouri farmers from whom we had rented pasture waved at us as we passed them. I think they were glad to see our backs. To tell the truth, we were glad to put Missouri behind us.

The summer heat didn't seem as bad without the cows as our constant companions. At least there were less flies and dust. In a week we crossed back into Kansas near Baxter Springs. Shelby reined in next to me. "Think I'd better leave you here. I'm gonna ride off the trail for a while and meet you at the Arkansas River crossing." I understood.

Pecos noticed Shelby leave the trail. "Where's he goin' in such a hurry?"

"It's not healthy for his neck to spend any extra time in Kansas."

We wasted no time in Kansas, either. As we crossed back into the Cherokee Strip, an old friend met us. John Walking Bear rode up on his old gray mule. "You white men didn't get yourselves killed? I hope you sold the cattle and they didn't run away." He wheezed in laughter at his own joke. "Hey, toothless bald-headed white man, you got any tobaccy?"

"I figured you'd turn up, you ol' skunk eatin' buzzard, so I brought some extra tobaccy and a sack of oats for that ol' bag of bones mule."

We made camp for the night in a shady grove of trees with good grass for the stock and a clear small stream. The horses and mules were hobbled and grazing under Kyle's supervision while Jake helped Kelly get supper started. Old John supervised and talked their ears off. Kyle flagged to get my attention. "Boss, we got company." He pointed across the trail to the edge of the timber.

I looked up to see a dozen or more riders drifting out of the trees. They all wore pistols and had rifles across their saddles.

"Hello, the camp! I'm ridin' in." An average sized man in his twenties with long dark hair eased his horse toward camp. The others stayed just in the edge of the timber. "You men look like Texas drovers. Bet you're comin' back from sellin' cattle in Missouri."

"I reckon that's our business and not yours! What do you want?"

"I want y'all to drop your guns. Tell that kid on the horse to get off and come in. We're gonna talk about the price of cattle."

"The hell you say!" I grabbed for the reins of the stranger's horse, but before I could raise my hand, I was staring down the barrel of a cocked pistol.

"Step away from my horse, friend. Frank, you and the boys ride on in!"

From the woods behind us, a rifle cracked. The bullet kicked up dirt and rocks under the horse causing it to lurch sideways.

"Jesse, is that you?" a man's voice demanded from the trees.

"Hell yes! You tryin' to get me killed? Who are ya? Come out and show yourself."

"If I was tryin' to kill ya, you'd already be dead. What are you and Frank doin' pickin' on an old friend's outfit?"

"Who are ya?"

"I'm the man that's got a rifle pointed at your chest. This is James Shelby. Remember me, Jesse?"

"James Shelby? I shore do. Boys, its James Shelby."

"Now don't get too excited. These drovers are all friends of mine. All of 'em are good Rebs, too. I thought your war was just against Yankees, banks, and railroads."

The outlaws all laughed. "Yeah, mostly you're right. But we collect Yankee dollars wherever we find 'em." Jesse pointed his pistol at me. "Shelby, you better come in before your friend gets hurt."

"Drop it, Jesse. I ain't kiddin'!" A shot rang out from the trees. Jesse's horse squealed, reared up and fell over dead, shot between the eyes.

Pecos used the excitement to grab the fallen outlaw's pistol and saddle gun. Kelly ran behind the wagon and came back with an armload of guns. Pecos had the pistol against Jesse's head with the hammer back. Each of the boys had some kind of gun in their hands. The impressive double barrels of Kelly's twelve gauge were leveled at the riders across the road. "You no good egg-suckin' skunks ever seen what buckshot does to a man? Come get ya a little taste!"

Shelby walked in from the woods with a Henry repeating rifle. It shot fifteen .44 caliber slugs as fast as you could work the lever.

"I got it pointed at you, Frank. Drop your guns and ride in with your hands where I can see 'em. I ain't shy about killin' ya."

Jesse was struggling to get free from the dead horse. Pecos shifted the pistol and loosened the cinch on the dead horse. He kept the gun at point blank range on Jesse's head. "Git up, mister. Pull that saddle off if you want it. Your friends better drop their guns before my hand gits tired."

"Jesse, what do you want us to do?"

"Kinda obvious, Frank. Y'all throw your guns down. I'm the first one gonna get killed. Nobody try anything!"

Frank was the first to pitch down his guns and the others followed. Jesse got on his feet with his hands in the air. "No harm done, except to my horse." He held his hand out to Shelby.

To our amazement, Shelby lowered his rifle and shook hands with Jesse, and then Frank, as he walked up. "Howdy, boys. Ain't seen y'all since Baxter Springs. Still ridin' with the same bunch?"

"Yeah. The Coulter and Dalton boys are over there, and Bill Anderson, too. Y'all say howdy to our old friend, James Shelby. He was a wild one back in the day, wasn't he, boys?" Several rough look-ing men tipped their hats. "Sure sorry to have bothered you, Shelby. If we had knowed it was you, we would've come for supper."

"Y'all just leave us alone and we'll kinda forget we saw ya. I knew you to rob and murder, but I'll take you at your word. You'll leave us be?" They both agreed and shook hands with Shelby again.

"Kyle, bring that blaze face sorrel of mine up here and throw Jesse's saddle on him. Not every boy can say he saddled Jesse James' horse." Shelby and the James brothers seemed to think this was real funny. None of us were laughing. "Sorry I had to shoot your horse."

"Like I said, no harm done. I was plannin' to rob ya." With that, he swung up on Shelby's freshly saddled horse, motioned for the others to follow and they trotted out of sight.

———————

There were plenty of questions that night around the campfire. Shelby admitted his name was James Shelby, the younger brother of Confederate General Joseph Shelby. "I didn't like takin' orders from him, so I joined up with Quantrill. When I first met y'all I hadn't been with Shelby's Brigade that was headin' to Mexico. I'd deserted from Quantrill's bunch and was on the run. I hoped nobody would recog-nize me. I know you remembered me, Kelly. I saw it in your eyes. I recognized you, too, from Prairie Grove. You kinda stick out in a crowd."

"Darn right, I recognized ya. I sure didn't know you was Joe Shelby's brother. Where I come from he's a hero."

"And I'm not."

"Well, Quantrill sure ain't no hero. He's a murderin' thievin' sack of horse manure."

"Well, I rode with 'em for nearly a year before I got a belly full of it. The killin' at Lawrence and Baxter Springs made me sick. I watched for a chance and sorta just disappeared. The Confederate government revoked Quantrill's commission when he got to raidin' in Texas. Even sent Rebel troops in to run him off. They declared him an outlaw and all that rode with him; so did the states of Missouri and Kansas. I'm wanted dead or alive in Kansas."

We sat quietly by the fire. I finally broke the silence. "Shelby, I don't know what to think about your past. Since you been with us, you been a good man to have around. I reckon you saved all of us today. You're welcome to stay on with us as long as you like and don't turn outlaw." A murmur of agreement circled the fire. We turned in for the night with a lot on our minds.

The swirling green water of the Arkansas was low enough that the horses didn't even have to swim. The wagon and mules easily splashed across. Weeds grew on the sandbar. We left Old John waving goodbye on the north bank. He proved to be good company. We never saw another Indian all the way back to the Red River. I sure was glad to see that muddy red water again. We stopped at the trading post at Preston to catch up on the news and to let Kelly renew his supply of tobacco. Soon we passed through Dallas and kept pushing south toward Waco. We made it back to Captain Tyus' ranch by the middle of September. The next day we rode into Waco to visit the Cattleman's Bank. They had adequate coin to honor everyone's bank drafts. The Captain suggested I might want to take only what we needed and leave some of the rest on deposit. They gave me blank drafts that I could use to draw the money at other places.

Kyle left us here, taking his string of horses home with his pockets full of silver dollars. He had proved a good hand. Levi and Luke headed out for home. It had been quite an adventure for them, but they had pulled their weight. Shelby said he wanted to travel for a while, but would be back in time to start cow work in the late fall. He took the saddle horse he was riding and two spare horses. He didn't say where he was going and we didn't ask.

"Well, Aaron. I'm anxious to get home to see my wife and kids. I appreciate the job. I hope I can cook for your next drive."

"Kelly, you were the 'wise old man' when we needed it. You're as good a camp cook as I ever saw. You can bet we'll get word to you for our next drive." Kelly mounted his gray draft horse and headed back to Hunt County.

Captain Tyus frowned. "Boys, I overheard Luke and Levi saying something about the James gang and Shelby. Did you have a little excitement?"

"Yessir, we did. We had kinda suspected Shelby had a little somethin' in his past he wanted to keep to hisself. Turns out his real name is James Shelby, brother of General Joseph Shelby. Instead of riding with his brother's brigade, he fell in with Quantrill's bunch. He was with 'em at Lawrence and Baxter Springs. He's wanted for murder, dead or alive in Kansas and Missouri. The James gang tried to rob us north of the Arkansas, but Shelby was hid out in the woods with a Henry rifle. He shot ol' Jesse James' horse dead out from under him, and made Frank throw down his guns. We got their pistols and rifles, while Kelly grabbed the guns from the wagon. If it hadn't been for Shelby, we'd lost all our money for sure, and likely our lives, too. The darnedest thing I ever saw was when Shelby walked out and shook hands with 'em and they had a good talk. They apologized for tryin' to rob any friends of Shelby, and then Shelby gave Jesse his best horse to make up for the one he shot."

"Saved me from gittin' bit by a rattler, and saved Luke from drownin' in the Arkansas."

"That surely is a strange story and a strange young man. I need to bring you boys up to speed on Texas politics while you were gone. General Throckmorton, as good an old Rebel as there ever was, got elected governor. Texas sent one man to the United States House of Representatives and two to the Senate, all good old Confederates. President Andrew Johnson declared the rebellion was over in Texas.

We elected a state legislature, too. They refused to take any action on the Thirteenth Amendment."

"Whoa, Cap. What's that?"

"Sorry to get ahead of you, Pecos. That's the amendment to the United States Constitution that forever makes slavery illegal in the whole country."

"I thought they done that June 19 last year."

"That was a presidential decree; this is an amendment to the Constitution. They did vote to confirm that the Confederacy was forever ended, nullified the Act of Succession, and voided all Confederate debts."

"So those vouchers we been holdin' and our Confederate paper money is worthless."

"There was also a proposed Fourteenth Amendment that would guarantee all people equal protection under the law. They declined to ratify that."

"What's that all about? I don't know any more about it than Pecos."

"That would give all the freed slaves the same rights as whites. That didn't get too far. They did adopt laws regulating the conduct of Negroes called the 'Black Codes.' Oh, the Yankees changed the military commander to General Charles Griffin. I don't know a thing about him."

We discussed the situation for a while and decided it could be worse. Little did we know that it soon would be much worse than we had ever imagined.

8

Gathering mavericks on the Brazos

THE FALL OF 1866 WAS SPENT gathering crops and tending the home raised cattle. The crossbred bulls produced a nice crop of calves with the longhorn cows. The former cane busters had become much more civilized and rarely tried to kill us anymore. Shelby came back right before Christmas. He offered no explanation and we asked for none. Mother and Noah had been glad to get their share of the cattle sales money. Momma used some of hers to keep us supplied with coffee and sugar. Pecos and I had more money than we had ever seen. Sheriff Moore and Mr. Morgan had been glad to get their bank drafts. The influx of real money helped all of us. The sharecroppers had done a good job. They planned to winter there and crop with us again next season.

Pecos, Shelby, Noah and I set up cow camp where the Camino Real crossed the Brazos. This was the same place where we had our first stampede last year. Pecos had blamed it on evil spirits. The place did have a dismal haunted quality about it. What had once been a prosperous little community before the war was nothing but a skeleton

74

of a dead town. I didn't particularly like it here, either, but this was where the cattle were. We used the remains of the four cabins and palisades that had once been a small fort. We would use the central area for our holding pen. We took our meals together in one cabin, but at night each slept in a separate cabin with loaded rifles. The doors were barred and the shutters closed. If we had Indian trouble, we would be ready, for the Comanche and Kiowa still raided down this far down the Brazos.

We started our cow hunt south of the Camino Real. We had built a sturdy rail fence two hundred yards along the river to keep them from jumping into the Brazos to swim away. There was also an angled wing fence that would direct them toward the pen. We had good luck with yoking the wild cattle we roped to oxen. It was a dependable method, but it was pretty slow. This season, we planned to just drive them into the catch pen and only use the oxen on any that were too wild to handle.

The hot breath from our four best brush-busting horses hung in the cold, still, morning air and looked like dragon's breath. Frost sparkled from the last few leaves clinging to the trees and on the winter-cured grass. Crashing in the brush and cane ahead of us signaled we had found the right place. We nudged the horses north along the dense thicket along the Brazos. I rode on the flank nearest the prairie. Shelby took the river flank, with Noah and Pecos between us. We saw cattle of all colors. There were steel gray grullas, brindles, blue-speckled mulberries, red-spotted sabinas, and every possible combination. We kept the brutes moving slowly, but relentlessly. An old outlaw bull turned on Pecos.

"Look out!" Shelby yelled. A black bull carrying wide upturned horns charged at Pecos with murder in his eyes. The razor sharp white tip of the bull's left horn ripped his horse in the belly. The horse screamed in terror and pain as blood and intestines poured from the gaping wound. Pecos went down hard, stuck under the dying horse. The bull turned his rage on the trapped cowboy. His wide horns swept across his chest, tearing his shirt off and opening a shallow cut.

Three shots rang out in rapid succession from Shelby's Henry at close range. The .44 caliber bullets slammed into the bull's head. His massive form collapsed on top of the still struggling horse. Another shot from the rifle stilled the thrashing horse. Before Noah and I could get there, Shelby undid the front and back cinches on Pecos' saddle. He grabbed him by the shoulders and pulled him free.

"You alright?"

"I ain't sure yet. That cimarrone ruined my fancy shirt. How's that cut on my chest look?"

"I've cut myself worse shavin'. You'll live."

"Thanks."

"Don't mention it. Y'all have had my back. I take care of my friends."

"I sure wouldn't want to be one of your enemies."

Shelby slipped the bridle off the dead horse and handed it to Pecos. "Let's git you remounted. We got work to do."

We caught a spare horse and helped Pecos get him saddled. "You need help gettin' on, Injun boy?"

"That'll be the day!" He sprung on the horse and rode toward the thicket with the tatters of his shirt flapping in the breeze.

_____

We could hear quite a few cattle walking north in the brush ahead of us. This time, Noah was on the river side of the thicket. A group of about twenty head jumped in the river swimming hard to get away. He spurred his horse into the cold water. The big bay was a strong swimmer, even with a man on his back. Cowboy and rider made it to a sandbar, and then loped to get ahead of the cattle. The mavericks hesitated at the sight of a rider on their flank. He pulled out his Colt Navy .44, which he had managed to keep dry. The five shots echoed up and down the river, sending the cattle swimming hard toward the east river bank. Noah and his horse had saved the day. As the big bay jumped back into the swirling water, Noah slipped off his back and held on to his tail to give the horse a break. They were both dripping wet and shivering when they got back to the bank. We caught him a replacement while he poured water out of his boots. He didn't have any extra clothes, so he just had to "cowboy up" until the day was over.

As we drew close to the wing fences and catch pen, we slowed down to a walk and gently pressed them away from the cane break. We allowed them to leave the safety of the brush and headed them along the river road. The oxen were standing in the open space inside the palisade. The longhorns saw them and headed toward the large make-shift catch pen. We backed off and they trotted into the enclosure like milk cows. Noah rode up and closed the heavy gate.

We spent the next week sorting and working the cattle. The bulls were castrated and all of them were branded with our brand, the rooftop AT on the left hip, and the road brand, an upside down T, on the left ribs. One of the old barren cows didn't look too healthy.

"I bet she's got the holler horn. Only way to treat it is to saw off the horns down to the quick."

"Pecos, you think that really works?"

"I seen it work before. What do we have to lose? She ain't gonna make it up the trail in the shape she's in."

After we had branded her and treated her for ticks, we secured her extra tight and sawed off about a foot of the ends of her long corkscrew horns. She squalled and bawled as we sawed through the thick old horns. We used a hot iron to cauterize the bleeding. She got up snorting, slinging blood and snot. We'd have to wait to see if it did anything more than make her mad.

———

Our next hunting trip took us north up the Brazos about eight miles. This run was a lot easier than the south had been. There were no killer bulls and no swimming escapes. The cattle trotted along pretty peacefully toward the new riverside and wing fences. The catch pen was now opened to the north. We pushed about one hundred and fifty cattle into the pen. We discovered we had eleven branded cows with nursing calves. These we chased back into the thicket. The cattle gathered from the south had settled enough they grazed peacefully in the rail fenced pasture near the cabins. We worked the new cattle and gradually released them to join the other cattle. As the castrated bulls healed, they seemed to adopt a gentler outlook on life. We had a total of one hundred and seventy-three stags, thirty barren market cows, eighty good young cows, along with several young heifers to add to the herd, and dozens of nice steer calves we would market as two year olds.

The four of us pushed the small herd forty miles in three days back to our land across the Navasota. They readily blended into the existing herd. The cow we had treated for the hollow horn we had named "Stubbs," and she had quickly shown she was the boss cow. The cattle fattened on the good winter grass, supplemented with whole cotton seed.

_____

Sheriff Moore rode to Centerville about twice a week to report to the county sheriff. He always brought back any mail for Navasota Crossing. There was a letter for me from Joseph McCoy, post-marked Abilene, Kansas.

> Aaron,
> I will cut right to the point. The Missouri legisla-
> ture has finally closed the state to Texas cattle. Other
> herds had not been treated for ticks and many local
> cattle died everywhere they contacted Texas cattle. A
> Scots Irish and Cherokee trader named Jesse Chisholm
> has blazed a trail through the center of the Indian
> Nations to a new railroad and cattle receiving depot
> at Abilene, Kansas. The trip will be shorter than the
> trail to Sedalia, and I have excellent facilities there. I
> would very much like to buy the quality of cattle I got
> from you last year. Please tell the Dawsons, Carters,
> Shepards, and Kelly Webb I will take any cattle they
> drive with yours. Of course, I have communicated this

to Captain Tyus also. Please write or telegraph me in
Abilene if you will be bringing a herd up the new trail
this year.
Your friend,
Joseph McCoy

9

March 30, 1867, Groesbeck, Limestone County, Texas

The Iron Clad Oath

THE IRON-RIMMED BUGGY wheels ground to a stop at Marcus' house in Groesbeck. "Good to see ya, Cap!"

"Hello, boys. Is there any coffee in the house?"

The hot coffee steamed the lenses on his cold spectacles before he set the cup down. "Well, I've got plenty of news, most of it bad."

Pecos and I exchanged nervous glances. "What's goin' on, sir?"

"The loyalty oath we took after the surrender to support the Constitution of the United States and never take up arms against her again has been replaced with a new 'Iron Clad Oath.' You have to swear that you never took up arms against the United States or served in an elected or appointed Confederate office, or gave any support to those who did."

"Shoot, that takes out every person I know. What does it mean to us?"

"You won't be able to vote, serve on a jury, or hold office. You have lost your basic rights as citizens." We sat in silence absorbing what he had said. Marcus got up and poured generous amounts of whiskey in our coffee.

"That's not all, either. Congress replaced the Presidential Reconstruction Act with the Congressional Reconstruction Act. Our representatives and both senators have been sent home. Throckmorton has been removed as governor, and our state legislature has been vacated. The south is now divided into five military districts. Ours is administered out of New Orleans by General Sherman himself." Pecos expressed himself in words not to be repeated, even though I agreed with him myself. "General Griffin in Galveston is now military governor of Texas. All the Negroes have been granted the right to vote, hold office, and serve on juries. The new Texas legislature must ratify the Fourteenth Amendment before it can be readmitted to the Union."

"Cap, if no old Rebs can hold office, what kind of government are we gonna have?"

"Negroes, carpetbaggers and Unionists."

"Oh, Lord." Pecos groaned. Captain Tyus was just full of good news.

"There's more. The Lipan Apache launched a major raid along the San Saba River. They killed any white settlers that didn't fort up and drove off over ten thousand head of livestock. The Yankee troopers didn't feel the need to respond."

I smiled at him. "Don't you have any good news?"

"Yes. I guess this other is all pretty gloomy. I got a letter from Joseph McCoy, as I believe you did. He's got a new shipping center set up in Abilene, Kansas. There is a new trail marked through the Nations all the way to Abilene. We can sell all the cattle we want and hunker down until times get better."

Bad times. We thought we were in bad times now. It was just the beginning of evil days to come.

Mother asked us to move her house to a small farm next to Marcus in Groesbeck. She felt pretty lonely at Navasota Crossing. I can't say I blamed her as it was pretty short on folks over there. I told her we would sure try to get it done, but I didn't have a clue how.

Shelby took to disappearing at night and coming back on a tired horse. He could have been courting, but a man usually doesn't need a revolver and rifle for that, or wear out a horse. We suspected he was up to no good, but left it alone. We had heard of colored soldiers who got caught away from their units being found hung. There was talk that it was the work of a new group known as the Ku Klux Klan. We avoided the topic and never mentioned it in front of Shelby. It was best not to know some things.

————————

Letters arrived that the Dawsons would have a small herd to Navasota Crossing by May 1. Kelly Webb sent word he would be there by then. There would also be Morgan and Moore cattle to throw in with ours.

The Shepards and Carters were sending cattle to Captain Tyus' place by May 12. There was plenty left to do. Noah got the wagon serviced and provisioned with anything Kelly had put on the list. We were all glad to see he ordered plenty of flour. Pecos and Shelby put in some time shining up those horses we would be taking to Kansas.

Logan Morgan built a special cook's box to fit in the back of the wagon. It had drawers and bins that latched closed. Hinged to the bottom was a heavy oak table that dropped down into place when it was needed. The whole contraption was made water and dust tight, and fitted with a special waterproof canvas cover. He made a canvas tent fly that extended back about twelve by eight feet to give the cook a little shelter from the sun or rain.

Pecos and I had bought Henry repeating rifles like Shelby's gun. They fired a .44-40 rimfire brass cartridge. We had seen firsthand how useful it could be. I sent a telegram to Mr. McCoy to expect us from mid-August to the first of September. We had never been up this trail and didn't know what to expect.

By May 1, our crew was ready to go. The dawn broke with a red sun piercing the last of the night's purple sky. As it was fully light, the eastern horizon was painted in red and pink. "Red sky at mornin', feller take warnin'."Kelly said as he loaded the wagon.

"Do you really believe that's true?" Logan asked.

"Seems like more often than not there's somethin' to them old sayin's."

Michael Dawson walked over where his sons were loading their bedrolls into the wagon. "You boys work hard and don't give Aaron and Kelly too much trouble." He glanced at me. "Aaron, I brought you one hundred and sixty-three cattle, ten horses, and two knuckleheads."

"They're pretty salty, Mr. Dawson. They did good last year and are taller and stronger than last year. We need to fatten Matt up. He looks like a string bean growing up a pole. You still gonna ride along to the first camp with Sheriff Moore, Mr. Morgan and Noah?"

"I think so. It'll be fun."

————————

"Get movin' you blue-backed, yellow-bellied good for nothin' crow bait!" Kelly cracked the long whip over the strong backs of our four best bay mules. The wagon lurched forward with the trace chains jangling. Jake pushed up the twenty spare horses, including Kelly's enormous draft horse. As the cattle started out of the pasture, down the Camino Real and across the river ford, one old cow gradually worked her way through the other cattle to her place at the front of the herd. It was "Ol' Stubbs" in all her glory, fat as a tick. We had contributed four hundred and eleven cattle to the herd. The Sheriff and Mr. Moore had added one hundred and eighty-two. Kelly had actually contributed ten head from his own little herd. Counting the Dawson's cattle, we had seven hundred and sixty-six head.

All that first day the clouds built behind us. The wind shifted to the southeast carrying the scent of rain. A low rumble of thunder could be heard in the distance along with faint flashes of sheet lightning. The cattle seemed unsettled and trotted a little faster west along the road.

Kelly and Jake had pulled off the road far enough ahead to get supper started. The horses were grazing hobbled in tall grass near the road. We bedded the cattle in a lush stand of prairie grass south of the road.

"Chow's up! Eat it now before I throw it out!" Kelly's hollering sounded just like old times. Jake served bacon, cornbread and pinto beans seasoned with salt pork. There was all the coffee we could drink. We had finished and just thrown the dirty dishes in the wreck pan when the thunder grew much louder. A blinding flash of lightning crashed near the herd. The top of an oak tree smoldered where the lightning had hit. The clacking together of horns rattled as over seven hundred cattle jumped to their feet.

Jake trotted up with his horse saddled, leading Kelly's big horse, as the rest of us started tightening the cinches of our own horses. The wind suddenly blew cold down from the tops of towering thunderheads, followed by fat heavy raindrops. As the wind rose, the rain came in horizontal sheets. Lightning flashed inside the clouds and the thunder grew into a continuous deafening rumble. Blue forked lightning crashed behind the nervous herd. They were off to the races. "All hands and the cook!"

I led the riders on the south side of the herd and Pecos led the north group as we galloped down the road to draw even with the herd. We gained on the leaders until I could see "Stubbs" out front. In the lightning flashes I could see that Pecos was across from me. The brutes seemed to be tiring from running in the muddy road. I spotted a large open prairie ahead of us on the north side of the road. I waved my hat at Pecos. He had seen it, too, and started to slowly drop back with his riders. When "Ol' Stubbs" was near the edge of the open prairie, I signaled the south riders to start to crowd in on the trotting herd. With pressure coming from the south, the herd veered north into the pasture. "Ol' Stubbs" slowed to a lumbering trot, then a walk as she went deeper into the wet grass. Within a quarter of an hour, the whole herd had slowed to a weary trot. The worst of the storm had passed on west of us, and only a gentle rain remained. The cows walked in a slow counter-clockwise circle. They started to grab bites of grass as they walked until at last, they were grazing. In an hour the tired animals began to bed down. It looked like we had survived in good shape.

"Kelly, you, Jake, and Matt bring up the wagon and remuda. Mr. Dawson, I know they would appreciate your help." I trotted over to Pecos. "I reckon they ran about five miles in the right direction. Makes for a mighty long day."

The sheriff rode up on a lathered horse. "Aaron, Logan and I haven't ridden like that since we served under your father in the Mexican War. This is not a job for an old man!" All the remaining riders huddled together and talked as we waited for the wagon and some hot coffee. He told the story of the Battle of Cerro Gordo where my father had led two hundred men in his Regiment of Scouts in a raid behind Santa Anna's line to capture his supply train. Finding a golden opportunity, they trotted to within two hundred yards and took well aimed fire with their rifles at the rear of the north corp of the Mexican army. In the confusion of battle, they went unnoticed until they had galloped to fifty yards and cut down on the enemy troops with a pair each of the powerful and deadly Walker Colts. The concentrated re-peating gunfire had panicked the north Corps. It started to collapse on the center. The Fourth Iowa Infantry saw the panic and charged the retreating troops in the flank. The Texans had snapped in fully loaded new cylinders in both guns and pursued the attack. With swarming troops to the front, left and rear, the length of the much larger line had collapsed in chaos. In the sheriff's weathered face I could see the image of a young man in his prime shining through the years. "Those were the days, weren't they, Logan."

The arrival of the wagon and our impatience for hot coffee brought an end to the stories I craved to hear, for I had not known my father. He had died when I was only a year old. Noah had no memory of him, either. By the time the coffee was on, it was time to start break-fast. None of us had slept all night. After biscuits and bacon, and plenty of coffee, Noah, Mr. Dawson and our two older friends were ready to start the trip home. I knew they must be tired, but Sheriff Moore and Mr. Morgan had a sparkle in their eyes I had never seen before. They rode off sitting straight in the saddle.

The rest of the trip to Waco was pretty quiet. We made good time and arrived at the Tyus place just before sundown on May 12.

The Captain met us in his buggy. "Hello, boys! Good to see you! How many head did you bring?"

"It's good to see you, sir. We've got seven hundred and sixty-six head. How about the others?"

"Luke and Levi drove in fifty-seven head and extra horses. Kyle Shepard got here with forty-one head of crossbreds and gentle longhorns and a string of good horses. I'm adding three hundred and forty-seven head. My tally puts us at one thousand two hundred and eleven. I hear the price is better than forty dollars a head."

We had our last woman-cooked food that night. Mrs. Tyus fed us fried chicken, ham, mashed potatoes and gravy, biscuits and apricot cobbler. It sure was good. It would be a long time before we would eat on a table. The Chisholm Trail lay before us.

10

The Road before Us

"HUP MULES! HUP! MOVE your overfed good for nothin' rears!" The reins slapped across their strong bay backs. They pulled into the newly repaired harness and set the wagon in motion. Jake slapped his hand on his chaps, setting the remuda into a trot following the wagon. I nodded to Pecos and Shelby. They put a little pressure on the herd and they stepped reluctantly forward. Before they were a quarter mile up the Dallas Road, "Ol' Stubbs" had shouldered her way to the front.

We made easy stages of ten or twelve miles a day, bedding the cattle in lush spring grass near clean water. There were typical May showers, but nothing like the first night. I rode up to the wagon to talk with Kelly. "I sure do like you havin' enough money for plenty of flour, coffee and sugar. Them boys are growin' fast and eatin' like hogs. Levi, Matt, Luke and Kyle all got holler legs. And I swear Jake's got half a dozen tape worms. I can't fill those boys up."

We made Fort Worth in good time. It was a town of three or four thousand people. The fort, now occupied by Negro soldiers, still dominated the hill above the river. Kelly saddled his big horse and rode into town to get a few supplies and some extra tobacco. He chewed it like a cow chews cud. Shelby, Matt, Pecos and I rode into town for a quick drink, but Shelby got into a fight with a Yankee officer and got us all thrown out of town. Seeing there were plenty of blue coats, we didn't argue too much.

The country northwest of Fort Worth was less settled than the country farther south. The Kiowa raided across the Red River and the Comanche swept east from the Double Mountain Fork of the Brazos. Livestock and isolated ranches were in constant danger. We armed each drover and doubled our night watch. It would mean less sleep, but maybe we could hang on to our cattle and our hair.

"Montague County sure is good lookin' cattle country, ain't it, Aaron."

"Yeah, real good, Pecos. Still a little too close to the Injuns to suit me."

North of the Nocona Bend of the Red River we picked up some more tobacco for Kelly and some odds and ends at Red River Station. We pushed along the trail to the edge of the river. Pecos rode the crossing to check the river bed. "It's firm; no quicksand. Water's down. They won't even get their tails wet."

Crossing the Red was uneventful. We bedded the cattle down about three miles north of the river in open pasture with scattered stands of oaks and pine. We continued to carry our guns and kept a double watch. This was dangerous country. Shelby, Luke, Levi and I rode in for breakfast. Kelly and Jake were puttering around the fire. We were within a hundred feet of the wagon when we heard a horse nicker in the trees west of the trail. "Pull up, boys!" I slipped my Henry out of the scabbard. Seeing my alarm, Shelby retrieved his rifle and the boys pulled their Colts. "Hello the camp! Kelly, wake up the boys and grab the guns. We got company to the west."

The camp sprang to life. Kelly pulled his double-barreled twelve-gauge from the wagon. Pecos was up in his summer drawers holding his Henry and strapping on his Colt. Kyle and Matt stood near their bedrolls, Colts in hand. Jake had fished his pistol out of the chuck box and crawled under the wagon to fight from cover.

A dozen Indians galloped out of the woods heading for our picketed horses. We dug in the spurs to get there first. It was just now light enough to see them clearly. Shelby pointed, "They're Kiowa. Look at the hair, one long thick braid over one shoulder."

"Shelby, I've seen you do it. Shoot their horses." We both fired and two of their ponies went down squealing in pain. We fired again and Shelby dropped another horse.

"Why ain't we shootin' them?"

"Maybe if we just kill a few horses, they'll leave. If we kill some of them, the whole tribe may be on us." As the remaining nine mounted Kiowa bore down on us, we shot two more horses. They continued to gallop in, turning their attention to us. Arrows whizzed by, one lodging in the swells of my saddle. "Forget the horses. Let 'em have it."

I heard a scream and saw Luke grab his leg. An arrow was sticking out at a crazy angle. He got his horse under control and thumbed back the hammer on his Colt. The Colt belched fire and the Indian who had fired the arrow fell dead from his horse. Shelby and I worked the levers of our Henrys as fast as we could. Levi emptied his Colt, but Luke now held his pistol unsteadily in both hands. The remaining mounted Kiowa galloped back across the trail, scooping up their unhorsed companions. There was enough light now that the camp could pick out targets. They fired at the fleeing Indians. Kelly fired off two rounds with his shotgun before reloading it. "They're over a hundred yards away. You can't hit them with the shotgun!" Matt argued. "Ha! Yeah, but they don't know that!"

We caught a glimpse of them fleeing to the west. Pecos and Matt trailed them a while to make sure they were gone. "Shoot, I burned the biscuits! Sorry, boys. I was a little distracted."

Levi helped Luke down from his horse. The arrow had given him a flesh wound in the outer thigh pinning him to the saddle by his pants. Levi wiggled the arrow loose from the saddle, and then helped him get his britches off. I cleaned it with whiskey. "Whoa! That hurts!"

"Sorry, pard. This could have been a lot worse. You got shot by a Kiowa arrow, then shot and killed the Indian! You're gonna be tellin' this story the rest of your life. You can carry that arrowhead around for good luck."

"Kelly, let's just grab a cup of coffee and some jerky. I want to get the herd on the trail! We gotta git as far from here as we can in one day." The bedrolls disappeared into the wagon and fresh horses were saddled. "Jake, you make sure that pistol is loaded. Keep the horses closed up tight to the wagon. Pecos, you and Shelby keep 'Ol' Stubbs' right behind the horses movin' at a trot. There ain't gonna be any grazin' on the trail today."

I swung wide of the herd and rode up a bald hill east of the trail. I couldn't see anything moving for a long way. I didn't see a thing and I didn't see or smell smoke. I trotted up the trail and didn't see anything. I turned my powerful brown horse around and rode all the way back to the drag. The Carter boys were keeping things closed up tight and had their pistols strapped on. Luke was no worse for the wear. I dropped back down the trail, but didn't find any sign we were being followed. The whole Kiowa attack had happened so fast, it was just now starting to sink in. I noticed my hands were shaking. Whether a man was wearing feathers or a blue uniform, I didn't much like him trying to kill me.

After a few more nights working double guard, we were so tired we dropped back to just two men on duty at a time. I looked hard for Indian sign, hoof-prints, campsites and smoke: nothing. "Pecos, what do you think?"

He shrugged. "They don't call this Indian Territory for nothin'." I just smiled. He could say a lot in a few words.

We reached Rock Creek Crossing. It was obvious that it was a frequently used campsite. There was clear water and plenty of grass. As we bedded the cattle down for the night, Kyle spotted a lone man on horseback heading south down the trail, followed by a pack train of a dozen mules. He looked peaceable enough.

"Howdy. Name's Jesse Chisholm. Mind if I share your camp?"

His face was like weathered rawhide with piercing blue eyes. We invited him to get down and join us. Everybody made their way around to meet him.

"Jesse Chisholm. You was the one that blazed this trail."

"Ah, the Indians have been usin' this trail before a white man ever set foot in America. I just marked it off where it's easier to see."

"I figured you was a cattleman."

"Ha! Not me. I don't mind eatin' 'em when I can't get buffalo, but I don't care about ownin' 'em. I been a trader for a long time. Y'all need anythin'?"

Kelly stepped away from his cooking. "You got any tobaccy? Never know when a man might run out. Sell me a dollar's worth. I'm cookin' bacon, biscuits and gravy."

"Hope you don't burn the durned ol' biscuits." Jake laughed.

I turned to talk with Chisholm. "We had a run in with about a dozen Kiowa about a day north of the Red River. We drove them off."

Chisholm's face clouded. "That would be part of Santanta's bunch. They're as bad as a sack full of snakes."

"What's it look like north of here?"

"Green. Plenty of water. Purty peaceable, too." Kelly called us to eat. We talked and drank coffee way into the night. "Them was mighty fine groceries, Ol' Biscuit."

Kelly returned a tobacco stained toothless grin. "It's nice to be appreciated. A fella burns the biscuits one time because of them Kiowa, these boys just won't let it go."

We never did see Jesse Chisholm again, but I don't think any of us ever forgot him. The trail continued north with just a little east in it. The grass was good and there was plenty of water. He had said we were the first herd up the trail. I guess he was right, because I never saw any kind of cattle sign.

Luke healed up nice with a dandy little scar. At the slightest invitation he would drop his pants to show it off. "Them Injuns was swarmin' all around us. One of 'em rared back and put an arrow right in my thigh. It stuck through me right into the saddle. I pulled my Colt and shot him dead off his horse." That was Luke's story and he was stickin' to it. Levi made him a leather thong to tie that arrowhead around his neck like a medal.

There was a cluster of houses and a trading post at Silver City, but it sure wasn't much to brag about. We had more supplies in the wagon than they did in the store. Kelly bought eggs, butter, and fresh vegetables from a local farmer. We found a decent place to stop and bed the cattle. Kelly fixed boiled mustard greens seasoned with salt pork, a large pot of pinto beans, and enough fried cornbread and butter to feed an army. Kyle was really enjoying the cornbread as the butter ran down his fingers. "Biscuit, this is the best cornbread I ever ate."

"I didn't think you liked it. That's only about your fifteenth piece. You better save room for dessert: wild plum cobbler, made with plenty of sugar."

"I tell you what; I've been cravin' somethin' fresh and green all summer. Those greens are good! Jake, would you pass me a bowl of cobbler?" I pleaded.

"The children of Israel couldn't have had manna that tasted better than this cobbler." I ate three helpings washed down with coffee with a little sugar and fresh cream.

"This beats that fancy dinner we had in Sedalia last year, and there ain't no ersters, either." Jake laughed.

There wasn't much about Silver City to remember, but for years we would talk about "Biscuit's Banquet."

At Caddo Springs, a small delegation of Caddo Indians came to ask for their grazing fee. They spoke good English. They wanted either two steers or fifty dollars. Pecos and I tried to negotiate. They were friendly, but knew the value of the steers compared to the cash. We gave up bargaining. I counted out fifty fat silver dollars. They gave me a carefully written receipt. "The grass and water are good ahead. No bad Indians. Watch for quicksand on the Cimarron." I thanked them and plopped the stack of coins in their hands.

We travelled on to the Dover Stage Stand on the Cimarron. The few folks there seemed glad to see some new faces, but we didn't have any news and neither did they. I checked the river crossing myself and found it solid enough. Kelly made it across with the wagon without any trouble, as Jake did with the horse herd. "Ol' Stubbs" was the first cow in the river with the others following. The current of the river caused the cattle to slowly drift a little farther downstream. By the time the tail-end of the herd was exiting the river, they were about a hundred yards from where they had entered.

It was here we got our first taste of quicksand. Half a dozen steers got stuck. Luke and Levi managed to get their horses safely across and had roped two of the cattle. They couldn't budge them. Matt, Shelby, Pecos and I each caught one and pulled without success. Kelly walked up with a shovel. "I seen this before. Their back ends are stuck. You can pull 'til their heads come off, but you ain't gonna git 'em out. Here, I'll show ya. Come on with me Jake and Kyle." They peeled down to their one piece summer drawers. They waded out into the murky water, feeling their way to avoid the quicksand. "Levi, you and Luke get some more lariats and be ready to rope any of us that git in trouble. A man can die in this stuff."

Kelly eased down behind the nearest steer, a big thick mulberry. He took the shovel and sunk it in the quicksand below the brute's knee. "Aaron, ease him some slack in the rope. If he turns to fight me, you pull him up hard." He steadily pulled backwards on the shovel causing a slurping sound. With the suction broken, the steer jerked his knee up and struggled to find footing. Kelly moved the shovel behind the other hind leg. As the suction released, the steer kicked and bawled and worked his leg free. I applied a little traction on his horns with the rope and he had all four feet on something solid. He lurched forward and was out of the water. He was so tired, he walked about fifty feet and lay down. Kelly moved on to the next steer. It was a big brindle that Pecos had roped. Kelly got him loose, but after only a few feet of forward progress he bogged down again. He handed the shovel to Kyle. "Time to learn, junior." Kyle used the shovel to get the left leg free, but when he tried on the right, the shovel slipped and he fell backwards in the muddy water. We all laughed at him, but he had released the steer which stood shaking off water on the bank.

They continued until there was just one steer left, a runty line-back dun. "Jake, this 'uns yours." The steer came loose easily enough, but when he was freed, he came at Jake with his corkscrew horns. Jake jumped back. The tip of the horn barely missed his head. Matt jerked the slack out of the rope and dragged the steer far enough he wouldn't hurt anybody. Biscuit, Jake and Kyle were worn out; I boiled a pot of coffee and passed around a sack of jerky and hard tack.

At Buffalo Springs we found a good place to make camp. An old man on a thin gray mule rode up to camp. "You white men ain't aimin' to cross the Strip without payin' me are ya?"

"John Walking Bear! You're a long way from home."

"Naw, the Strip's my home. Anyway, they ain't no cattle comin' up the Shawnee Trail so I collect here. You're the first herd up the trail."

"Alright, here's your thirteen dollars and a pouch of tobacco. Any of that money get back to the tribe?"

"Enough that they ain't fired me yet. Thanks for the tobaccy. Where's Chief Bald Eagle of the Tall Man Tribe?"

"Hello, you ol' buzzard eater. You here for some of my good cookin'?"

"I sure didn't come for your looks. That's why I showed up at supper time."

We visited while we ate. John stuffed himself. Jake dug around in the wagon and poured a pan of oats for the old mule. "You're gonna spoil him, Jake."

"Looks to me like he could use some spoilin'."

"We met Jesse Chisholm. He seems like a good man."

"Yeah, he is a good man. Did he tell you he was half Cherokee?"

"No, I guess he didn't."

"His momma was. He speaks Cherokee and most of the Plains languages. He's about the only honest man around here besides me."

We left the next morning. When we reached the Chikaskia

River, John said we were in Kansas. He turned back and said he'd look for us on the trip back. We crossed the little river near a grove of hackberry and cottonwood trees and made camp. In three days we were on the banks of the Arkansas. The river was wide and deep enough the stock would have to swim part of the way. Both the north and south banks were gently sloping here with enough rock so that it would not to be too slippery. I didn't find any quicksand, and I remembered to check downstream. We camped south of the river. The cattle put their heads down and started grazing in the lush river bottom. They had gained weight on the road, as we had hoped they would.

We waited until the sun was well up to start across the river. We didn't want to take a chance on the rising sun reflecting into the cows' eyes. The mules trotted right into the cool green water. They had to swim a little way, but soon found their footing and pulled the wagon across. Jake started the remuda into the Arkansas. He was in his summer drawers and bare-footed as we all were. The horses took the crossing without a hitch. "Ol' Stubbs" started in the water on her own, the rest of the herd following her. The current was not too strong and the herd didn't drift much. We had successfully crossed our second herd over the mighty Arkansas. Fortunately, today she showed us her kind side.

We were on the last leg of our drive now. There were mostly small creeks and streams from here to Abilene. Kelly rewarded us with another apricot cobbler. Matt and Jake pulled out their guitar and fiddle and entertained us until we fell asleep under the Kansas stars.

In a few days we were camped on the Solomon River, with Abilene on the other side. Joseph McCoy rode out to meet us. He brought cigars and a bottle of good whiskey. "Aaron, these are as good or better than the last herd I bought from you. There are plenty of crossbreds and all the cattle are in good flesh. You're the first herd to reach Abilene. I was going to offer you forty dollars across the board, but I'll make it forty-two as a bonus. I'll throw in the Chinese bath house and laundry, plus dinner on me. Will that work for you?"

"Yessir. We'll be ready to cross in the morning."

11

Trouble in Babylon

I HAD SEEN CITIES AND TOWN, big and small during the war, but I wasn't quite prepared for Abilene. It had a raw edge like moonshine whiskey. The railroad station and shipping pens dominated the dusty landscape. A huge black locomotive sat idly puffing black smoke as sweating workers filled its water tank and coal car. Stout empty pens built of thick uncured planks stretched along the tracks. The town, if you could call it that, was two streets crossing at a single intersection. The buildings were built of swelling, warping unpainted lumber. Some weren't anything more than tents with wooden floors. There was a substantial looking bank building with a brick front, but canvas walls and roof. Workmen scurried about with wheelbarrows of bricks and buckets of mortar. Wagons loaded with lumber and barrels of nails rolled behind sweating teams of draft horses. Roofing tin and all sorts of building materials were being unloaded from boxcars at the station. Chinese laundry women bent over steaming tubs of clothes. Gamblers and bartenders leaned back in chairs on the boardwalk, while "soiled doves" peered from behind upstairs curtained windows. It was going to be an interesting visit.

We circled the cattle wide of town and approached the pens. Joseph McCoy waited for us as promised. One of his agents, Pecos and I tallied the cattle. Our counts agreed at one thousand two hundred and eleven head of good Texas beef. "Aaron, that comes to better than fifty thousand dollars. That's a lot of money."

"That's a lot of work and trouble, too. Let's get to the bank."

The banker stood up and walked around his desk to greet Mr. McCoy. He didn't seem bothered by my sweaty clothes, greasy chaps, or boots and spurs. "You Texans will be the life-blood of Abilene. I'm very proud to meet you, Mr. Turner."

"Nice to meet you. I've been just Aaron most of my life. I lack a few months being seventeen. Aaron would be just fine."

Mr. McCoy looked up. "You're just sixteen! That means you were just fifteen last year in Sedalia. I never dreamed you were that young. You've bossed two herds up from Texas. I'm impressed."

"Mr. McCoy, I went off to war in '62 when I was twelve. I got captured and sent to prison camp when I was not quite thirteen, got released, and killed my first man at Chickamauga, and more than I want to talk about before the war was over. I saw and did things that kinda age a fella."

"I understand. Let's get you paid. How did the bank transfer and drafts work for you?"

"Just fine. I'll need enough coin to pay my drovers, resupply and some road money. I want about five thousand in hard money. The rest you can wire to Cattleman's Bank in Waco. I'll divide shares when we get home." I waited while they counted out the coin. A boy ran down the street with a telegram. We made small talk until he got back. The telegram he brought confirmed the deposit in the Waco bank.

"Seems like I heard you had a drover named Shelby. Is he related to General Joseph Shelby from Missouri? He is considered quite a hero there."

"Mr. McCoy, I don't mean to be impolite, sir, but we don't

believe in askin' too many questions. If a man wants you to know somethin', he'll tell ya. If he does his job, he's alright in my book. I've worked with the cowboy you call Shelby for two years; he's a good man to ride the river with."

Mr. McCoy and the banker looked kind of surprised, and then started laughing. "I'll never understand you old Rebs or Texans. I'm sorry. I didn't mean any harm. There is paper out on a young man named James Shelby who rode with Quantrill. He's wanted for murder in Kansas and Missouri; he's Joe Shelby's little brother. If that man were around here, he might want to make himself kinda scarce."

"I'm not sure what that has to do with us, but I'll keep it in mind."

"I still want to treat you and your men to the best of Abilene. Lunch is on me. I convinced old Chin Li to move here from Sedalia to Abilene; I've got things set up there, too."

———————————

Lunch was corn-fed beef steaks, yeast rolls, fresh vegetables and fried potatoes. We had cake, ice cream and coffee for dessert. We all ate like lions. Watching Kelly gum a steak was something to see. "Biscuit, this is nearly as good as your cookin'."

"Yep, and there ain't no ersters!" Jake grinned. "I guess Luke's hat is safe for now."

We got the same deluxe treatment at Chin Li's that we had in Sedalia. After we had been scrubbed, shaved and shined, we went shopping. A new brand of pants was on the shelves made of heavy blue denim with brass rivets at all the stress point. They had a leather patch sewed on the pocket that read "Levi Straus and Sons, San Francisco, California." The store clerk called them "Levi's." We all bought a pair or two except Kelly. They didn't make any that would fit him. We got factory made shirts, socks, drawers and nice felt hats. Kelly bought everything we needed for the trip home and plenty of tobacco.

I went down the street and bought some real pretty handmade silver-inlaid spurs with two inch twenty point rowels and jingle bobs.

Pecos got a similar pair with some four-leaf clover rowels. Shelby had asked me to pick out a pair for him. I found a set with silver stars on the outside shank and rowels made from Mexican five peso coins cut into stars. I never saw a fancier pair of spurs anywhere.

Shelby was really proud of them. I pulled him to one side. "Mr. McCoy said there is paper out on you for murder in Kansas and Missouri. There were posters up in town. You need to make yourself scarce. Catch up with us somewhere down the trail."

———

The next day, Pecos and Matt trimmed and shod all the horses and mules in preparation for our long trip home. A deputy United States Marshal rode out to our camp while we were packing the wagon. "You the trail boss?"

"Yessir. Name's Aaron Turner from Leon County, Texas." I tipped my hat and extended my hand.

"Oh, sorry. Jess Wayne Webb, deputy United States Marshal for eastern Kansas. Do you know James Shelby?"

"I know a fella calls himself Shelby, just Shelby. He came up the trail with us."

"Is this him?" He showed me a wanted poster marked one hundred dollars, dead or alive.

"Sheriff, this ain't a very good picture. You fellas recognize this man?"

Levi spoke up. "Yeah. I seen that picture before in a newspaper. That's U.S. Grant."

"No, it ain't. That's General Sterling Price. I seen him in Arkansas." Kelly grinned and spat tobacco a little too near the lawman's boots."

"Sorry, Sheriff. Looks like we ain't too sure."

"It's Marshal Webb. Deputy United States Marshal Jess Wayne Webb. You sayin' this ain't the man who rides with you?"

"Sheriff, I just said I ain't sure who you're lookin' for, or who is in that sorry picture."

"I want some answers from you, Turner. You're ridin' back into Abilene with me."

"Am I under arrest?"

"No, I just want you to answer some questions at my office."

"Kelly, you're in charge here until I get back. Pecos, you and Matt go find Mr. McCoy pronto and meet me at this Yankee lawman's office."

The marshal wasn't too friendly and I didn't have much to say. The boys showed up with Mr. McCoy, who was none too happy. "Marshal Webb, this man brought the very first herd up the Chisholm Trail from Texas to Abilene. You do remember that's why I built this town was to get cattle here from Texas? I paid him more than fifty thousand dollars, Mr. Webb. Right now he is the most important man in Abilene and you are treating him like a saddle tramp! If he says he isn't sure you're talking about the same man, then take his word for it. If you want to find this James Shelby, get looking for him!"

"Mr. McCoy, I think he knows somethin' he ain't tellin' me."

Mr. McCoy turned to talk to me. "Mr. Turner, this trail hand, known to you as Shelby, have you seen him commit any crime in Kansas?"

"No, sir."

"Have you ever seen Shelby commit a crime anywhere?"

"No, sir."

"Do you believe the likeness on this wanted poster is your drover, Shelby?"

"Sir, like I told the sheriff, that picture could be anybody from Jefferson Davis to President Andrew Johnson."

"Are you wanted in Kansas?"

"Well, I hope you want me here! But, no, I'm not wanted for any crime in Kansas, or any other dang place." Mr. McCoy and the boys just laughed. The marshal got red in the face.

"Marshal Webb, as Mr. Turner and his drovers return to Texas, I expect they will meet other herds on the trail. It would be most troubling if he told them Texas drovers could expect problems from the law in Abilene, since buying Texas cattle is the whole reason this town was built."

"I see your point, Mr. McCoy. There is a man wanted for murder. I'm just trying to do my job."

"I understand that. Questioning a man of Mr. Turner's stature at his camp was bad enough, but to bring him in for questioning is inexcusable."

"Mr. McCoy, the sheriff didn't arrest me. I came at his invitation. Of course, it is hard to turn down the request of a lawman. If he'll just leave us alone, I'll forget all about it."

"Alright, I guess I know all I'm gonna find out. I won't bother ya anymore."

"Matt, you ride out to camp and let John Walking Bear know I'll be along directly."

Matt frowned a minute. "Oh, sure, Aaron. I'm on my way."

"Sheriff Webb, to show there's no hard feelin's, I insist you let me treat you to a beer."

One beer turned into three, all enjoyed very slowly. Matt had caught my hidden meaning for Shelby to head to Buffalo Springs in the Cherokee Strip where we had camped with John Walking Bear. He had saddled a strong fresh horse, filled his war bag with food, and picked two other good horses for remounts. He was fifteen miles down the trail before the marshal left the saloon.

"Aaron, I think it might be wise for Shelby not to come back to Kansas."

I looked at Mr. McCoy and smiled, "Shelby who?"

———

We made good time on the return trip. We found Shelby camping at Buffalo Springs with John Walking Bear. "You boys been takin' it easy?"

"Yeah. Ol' John shot a fat doe a couple of days ago. We been eatin' good."

"How you sleepin', Shelby?"

"With one eye open, but a lot better in Oklahoma than Kansas."

We met half a dozen herds coming north on the trail. We camped with them when we could and swapped stories. Luke showed off his scar every chance he got. Some of the drovers had run-ins with Satanta and his Kiowa war band along the Red River. The Kiowa lost a dozen warriors when a fed up bunch of Texas cowboys had lit into them with pistols and repeating rifles. Maybe it would keep things quiet for a while.

It sure was good to see the Red River again. When we crossed back into Texas, I knew I was nearly home. We sure didn't let any moss grow on our saddles until we got to Waco. We telegraphed from Dallas we would be there in three days. Mr. Carter came to meet Luke and Levi. I wrote him a draft off the Cattleman's Bank while the boys talked his ears off. I sure was going to miss those two. Kyle Shepard's grandfather was waiting on him. I wrote him his draft, too, while I bragged on what a good hand Kyle had become. Matt and Jake didn't wait around long. They loaded their bedrolls, war bags and instruments on their spare horses. Matt took their bank draft and trotted off. Jake turned back to give Kelly a hug, then loped to catch his brother. "I sure am gonna miss that kid." Kelly complained.

"Yeah. He thinks a lot of you, too. You got a wife and a house full of kids back home in Hunt County." Kelly climbed up on his gray draft horse and clicked him into a slow trot. He turned and waved his hat to us, his bald head shining in the sun.

"Aaron, I want you, Pecos and Shelby to be my guests tonight. I want all the details of the trip. We'll eat and talk cattle and politics."

"Sounds good, Cap. I gotta ride in to Waco to the bank. I'll be back for supper." Shelby and Pecos rode along to keep me out of trouble. I drew out a pile of money in silver and gold coin, but left more on deposit at the bank adding a little to our nest egg. They were even crediting it with a bit of interest. It felt kinda nice when I walked in and they called me Mr. Turner.

Mrs. Tyus fixed us a really good supper and made a big pot of strong black coffee. We filled Captain Tyus in on the entire story except a little part about the marshal that I left out. He had quite a bit of news, too.

President Johnson had been impeached. He had been put on trial to be removed from office, but the impeachment failed by one vote. He was a Democrat and the Republicans distrusted him. They accused him of being soft on Reconstruction. From that time forward, the Republicans had increased their power and flexed their political muscle. "Boys, I'm afraid that the Republicans have grown strong enough to make things mighty tough on the South. It looks like bad days are coming."

12

Finding a future on the frontier

THE WAR HAD BEEN OVER FOR almost three years, yet peace proved elusive in Texas. Indian raids along the Red River had worsened in the fall of 1867. Finally, the puppet Yankee government had responded. They met with the warring tribes from southern Oklahoma at Medicine Lodge and negotiated a treaty. Unfortunately, Satanta had refused to participate.

The Federal troops finally realized the vulnerability of the Texas frontier to Indian raids. They responded by building a series of mutually supporting forts. They reached from Fort Richardson at Jacksboro to the wild and wooly Fort Griffin in Shackelford County on the Clear Water Fork of the Brazos. Next was the ill-named and ill-fated Fort Phantom Hill in Jones County. The wells never produced enough water to cover daily needs. Patrols sent out to haul in extra water were attacked by the Comanche, and the water wagons burned. Disease dogged the camp. Local lore held that the camp was built on an old Comanche burial ground, and the spirits of departed warriors disrupted the dreams of the soldiers stationed there. Finally,

Fort Concho was built at the confluence of North and South Concho. It blocked the traditional route of the Comanche from their Plains kingdom to the unprotected villages of northern Mexico. Unfortunately, it also marked the northern extreme of the range of the Lipan Apache. It was a dangerous place. These forts were manned with poorly trained Negro infantry. They were no match for their enemies in the field, but the forts provided a place for refuge and resupply. Their presence seemed to draw Comanche raids like lightning rods.

When we returned from Kansas I divided the proceeds. Mother, Noah, Pecos and I were equal partners and pocketed almost four thousand dollars each. Shelby worked for wages.

We ordered three Red Durham bulls from Georgia. They came by ship to Brazosport, then by riverboat up the Brazos. They were gentle and easy to drive. Their massive, muscular red frames should add a great deal of quality to the calves. We would keep a few of the best bull calves and most of the heifers.

Mother's sharecroppers had filled her corn cribs and root cellar. The smokehouse was full of salt pork, hams, sausage and jerky. Mother was very pleased, and the sharecroppers had more to eat and wear than they had their whole lives.

The creeks and river bottoms near Navasota Crossing had been pretty well worked out of cattle except for a few old outlaws. Pecos perked up. "There's still plenty of mavericks down in my old stompin' grounds on the upper Colorado where I was raised. Let's get some spare horses, a couple of pack mules and plenty of grub and go have a look."

The country east of the Brazos was like riding across our own back pasture, but once we were near the Colorado River, it started to look a little foreign to Noah and me. "This is my home country. I've missed it." As we got closer to the Colorado, deer and turkey were plentiful. We had fresh meat every day and saved our salt pork and jerky.

Once we struck the banks of the Colorado, we followed it in

a roughly west by northwest course into the less populated areas. The farther we travelled the more maverick cattle we saw. When we reached the junction of Pecan Bayou with the Colorado, the water was crystal clear. The bayou teemed with fish. As the stream angled away to the northwest, it opened up beautiful cattle country. The cold winter sky was filled with sandhill cranes, ducks and geese. In the broken prairie, scattered herds of shaggy buffalo grazed. Their breath hung in heavy wreathes of steam around their huge heads. Their grunts and bellows sounded wild and ancient. We continued to follow the clear water deeper into the wild unsettled Texas frontier. We kept our rifles across our laps and our Colts always at hand. This was Comanche country. Finally, we found the land of the longhorns. They were everywhere. Old bulls and young calves, grown cows, and yearlings were in groups of tens and hundreds. There were grullas, linebacks, mulberries, sabinas, duns and brindles. There were so many cattle we should be able to put together a market herd in no time.

There was a small clear creek that followed the ridge of hills that ran east to west for miles. We built a dugout into the south side of one of the hills overlooking the creek. Then we built a stout corral similar to the one we had built at home. It was tall, tough and tight. "Pecos, I love this country out here. A man has elbow room."

"You ain't gonna like it so much when the Comanche come callin'."

We decided we had done all we needed to do and planned to head home in the morning. Pecos looked concerned. "I'm gonna hobble the horses and mules inside the corral tonight. I got a bad feelin' we're in for company."

"What's the matter? Your Injun blood got you scared of evil spirits again?"

"Shelby, your silver dollar mouth is gittin' ahead of your two bit brain. You'd best shut it before I do." Shelby just laughed. I finished supper.

"Why does he do that? Them horses are penned up in the best corral west of the Brazos."

"I learned a long time ago not to ignore Pecos when he's got one of his feelin's."

After supper we settled down inside the dugout in our soogans. The door had a wool blanket tacked over it and the single window was covered with a dried deer skin. Clouds had moved in, darkening the sky. A coyote yelped in the brush to the south, answered by another near the corral.

Pecos sat bolt upright. "That's not coyotes. We got company."

We were immediately up on our knees, Henrys in hand, with Colts on our sides. Pecos pushed the edge of the blanket aside with the barrel of his rifle. An arrow plunged through the blanket, burying itself in the back wall. The horses nickered and the mules brayed. The corral gate, which faced the dugout, swung partially open and snagged. Loud whoops came from the corral as our uninvited guests tried to drive the stock out. There was a brief glance of an Indian pushing the gate open. A shot from Shelby's rifle knocked him backwards. A second Indian appeared, attempting to drive a mule through the gate. The mule balked, kicked backwards with both hind feet, and caught the thief squarely in the chest. Three arrows whistled into the window and door of the dugout. We levered several shots in their general direction. Hoof beats rang out to the west and south. The horses still nickered and squalled, but the mules had stopped braying. Then there was silence.

"Shelby, you got the window; Noah, take the door. Me and Pecos are gonna check things out." I passed around a box of cartridges for the Henry rifles. Silence. The clouds had thinned and a weak trickle of moonlight filtered through.

I rolled out the door and came up kneeling to the right of the dugout. Pecos did the same on the left. Nothing moved. Silence. I could hear my own heart beating. I signaled to Pecos. I sprinted to the corral and flattened myself against the rough wooden side. Nothing. Pecos waved his hand and ran to the corral fence on the opposite side of the gate. I could see a faint reflection on rifle barrels in the dugout. I eased toward the gate and pointed my rifle around the opening. Pecos followed suit on the other side. "You see anything?"

"Yep. Eight horses and two mules. No Injuns."

"I'm walkin' in. This is like steppin' in a washtub full of snakes. Cover me." I made my way around the inside of the dark corral. The horses and mules shied away from me, but calmed when they heard my voice. As the stock shifted, I got a good look across the corral. "All clear." Just inside the gate was a dark stain on the hard ground. A quick sniff confirmed the sickly sweet, sticky aroma of blood. "Pecos, come take a look. Blood, a lot of it."

He stepped into the corral. "Shelby, you got one of 'em. Guess they dragged him off."

"Let's make some coffee." I stirred the coals from supper into a nice glow and added some dry sticks to get it blazing. I didn't think a big fire would be a good idea. As soon as the coffee was boiling, I took it inside to drink. None of us slept. We leaned against the bare walls and talked.

"Noah, you remember how Corporal Payton and his brother picked off all those Yankee officers at Adairsville?"

"Yeah, that was some kind of shootin'. Were you where you could see it, Pecos?"

"Heck, yeah. They killed so many officers, they didn't know what to do or which way to run. Both the Payton brothers got it at Franklin."

Franklin. The name chilled me. I had been fourteen. Of the twenty-four thousand ragged men of the Army of Tennessee that had taken the field that afternoon, only seven thousand could answer roll call that night. The rest were dead or wounded. Of our company of one hundred and twenty men who had left Texas, Noah, Pecos, Pink, Captain Tyus and I were the only ones to ever see Texas again. We had unintentionally opened the graves of the ghosts of our past. Silence filled the small dugout.

As purple showed in the east, Shelby slipped out to revive some of the embers of our fire. "Y'all cover me just in case we have company." He tossed out the cold coffee and grounds and refilled the pot. As the fire danced, the sky lightened to pink. I joined Shelby to slice off some bacon. Once the coffee was boiling, Noah and Pecos came out. All four of us wore our Colts and had our Henrys within reach. The coffee and bacon were just what we needed. We warmed ourselves by the small fire as the sun broke the horizon.

Pecos grabbed his rifle. "Let's look around." There were two sets of drag marks in the corral. "I guess that mule nailed one, too." There were bloody stains on the cedar logs where they had been hoisted over the fence. We found signs where three horses had been tied to the south, and four to the west. "Even a Yankee officer could figure there were seven of them."

Our journey back home was uneventful. The wild beauty and tremendous potential of the country along Pecan Bayou stayed in the back of my mind.

———————————

"Aaron, are you boys going to move me to Groesbeck, or not?"

"Yes, Momma. Marcus found a little place real close to him. It's got three acres of garden and orchards, with seventeen acres of good pasture and a nice barn. There's a decent old cabin, but nothin' like this house. They want two hundred dollars for it." Mother went to the cupboard and counted out ten double eagles from the cookie jar.

"Buy it! I don't even need to see it. I can live in that little cabin until you get my house moved." I found Logan Morgan the next day to ask if it could be done.

"Sure it can. I'll help keep you organized. We'll take it down in order, mark the logs and put them back where they go in Groesbeck. I'll convert a wagon to haul the logs."

I kept the gold coins and mailed a draft to Marcus to buy the land. We loaded Momma's belongings into two wagons loaded to the top and pulled by four mules each. We left before daylight and didn't get there until after dark. We left the loaded wagons at the new place and rode the mules over to Marcus' house a quarter of a mile away. The next morning Momma, Mary Ann and little Alice started cleaning the cabin. They scrubbed the walls with turpentine and swept the floors. Alice complained the whole time, but a little swat from Momma stopped that. We moved her things into the cabin, but there wasn't much room left. The barn, stalls, hen house, corn crib and outhouse didn't need any work. There was a little farm equipment that sold with the place. I plowed, harrowed and listed the garden. At supper that night, wedged tightly in the little kitchen, she told us she wanted the house moved as soon as possible. Noah and I had met our match.

———————

Mr. Morgan used a pine log to link a front and rear axle salvaged from an old wagon. Both the front and rear axles would turn, making it possible to maneuver in tight places. There was no wagon bed, just some sturdy cross pieces and side stakes to keep the logs from shifting. Pecos, Shelby, Noah and I moved our things into the store. We took the roof tiles off the cabin and carefully stacked them in two regular wagons. We hauled them to Groesbeck, unloaded them, and marked off the foundation.

Pecos and Shelby got all the doors and precious glass windows and shutters down while we were gone. Mother said my father had the windows shipped in from New Orleans. All four of us took them to Groesbeck and spent a week digging the foundation footings for the house and back-filling those with rock, gravel and sand mixed with burned limestone and water.

We disassembled the house, numbered each log and stacked them in orderly piles. Once we got the logs down, we took up the sanded plank floor and the cypress floor joists. We loaded the special wagon so that we could get to the logs in the order we would need to unload them, with the foundation sleepers on the top of the first load. It took four trips to haul all the big logs, with the planks riding along in the regular wagon. Finally, we took down the chimneys and loaded the bricks in two wagons. Mr. Morgan went with us to direct the reassembly. Marcus and Pink joined us. Mother was boss of the job. She kept us working and had food ready on site so we wouldn't have to leave to eat. With all of us working, it took two weeks to put it all back together. It looked grand and Mother was thrilled.

We moved most of our things over to Groesbeck, too, leaving just enough at the store for four young bachelors to survive. Our work and life in Leon County was almost, but not quite, over. As we had for four generations, we looked ever westward for our future.

———

That summer a new state convention was held in Austin. Eighty percent of the delegates were Republicans. The Iron Clad Oath kept Confederate veterans, officials and their families from participating. The convention favored a strong national government at the expense of the rights of individual states. The new Constitution gave enormous power to the governor. He was given the power to appoint office holders at all levels of government from the state Supreme Court down to county hide inspectors and town sheriffs. All county courts were abolished; and they were replaced with district courts controlled by the governor. A poll tax was established for those few who could still vote. The new Constitution gave Negro men the right to vote, hold office, testify in court, file lawsuits, and serve on juries. Now, the old structure of pre-war Texas was gone. Those of us who had been part of Texas before the war found ourselves disenfranchised, denied the rights now granted to former slaves and Yankees. Our world had been turned upside down.

———

The new Constitution was adopted and enthusiastically enforced. The Republican Party was divided. The most extreme members bolted from the main party and formed the Radical Republican Party. They wanted every vestige of the Old South destroyed and placed under the heel of the victorious industrial North. They advocated breaking Texas into three smaller, more manageable states.

Jack Hamilton was elected governor. He had been a Unionist

before the war and a Republican now. He was a close ally of General J. J. Reynolds, the military governor.

In national elections, General Ulysses S. Grant, a Republican, was elected President. Texas sent two Republicans to the House of Representatives and two Republicans to the Senate. Our voices had been silenced. We had no part of the new government. We were a defeated people.

As if our misery was not complete, the summer rains failed us. The corn grew only four feet tall with one shriveled partially filled ear. The other crops suffered as well. Our pastures wilted, but we were stocked so lightly our livestock didn't suffer. We hadn't gathered mavericks and we didn't have enough home raised cattle to take up the trail to Kansas. We had done well, very well, with our cattle business and saved the profits. We dug up hidden stashes of silver and gold to buy sugar, flour, coffee and salt. If it became necessary, we could even buy corn. We clung closely to our family and friends. We clung to our faith in God. We clung to hope; hope that someday things would get better.

13

The Depths of our Despair

HEAVY, DEEP COUGHING came from the back bedroom. The unmistakable odor of camphor filled the hot cabin. Logan Morgan lay piled under quilts in a bed he had built himself. His gray unshaven face was beaded with sweat. The sheriff and I took off our hats. "Hello, Logan. Aaron and I wanted to check on you."

A heavy fit of coughing wracked the failing, frail body of our friend. "Hello, Tanner. Hello, Aaron." His voice was a crackling whisper, the death rattle.

"Sheriff Moore and I checked your stock this morning. You sure got some fine animals."

"Aaron, you know good as I do I'm not gonna get over this pneumonia. I'd I like you to buy out my half interest in the herd. My wife is gonna need the money. She's plannin' to move in with our son near Dallas. I want to ask you to lease the pasture and send her the rent until she sells it. Tanner, that sound fair to you?"

"That sounds real fair. The pairs are worth about ten dollars, the yearlings and other stock about five dollars a head. Ten cents an acre is about right on the rent. You're too tough to die, old friend. You're gonna be around a long time yet." The look in Logan's eyes betrayed the truth that he wouldn't.

———

Sheriff Moore was riding to Centerville to talk to the county sheriff. He had received a letter that a sorrel john mule had been stolen from a Negro sharecropper. It was branded OT on the left hip. Sorrel was a common color in horses, but not so much in mules. As he trotted his flea-bitten gray gelding north on the Centerville road, he noticed a colored man deep breaking a garden plot next to his cabin with a sorrel mule. When he turned in and tied his horse, he could see the OT brand. His badge shone in the daylight. "Boy, where'd you get that mule?"

"That ain't none o' yo bidness."

The sheriff slowly pulled his Colt and leveled it at the man's bib overalls. "There's a sorrel mule branded OT reported stolen. That looks like him to me. Where'd you get him?"

The big man stepped closer. "I found him." Before the old lawman could react, the accused man hit him hard across the head with a singletree, crushing his skull and killing him instantly. Three white freighters on the road saw the fatal blow. They captured the murderer and tied him inside a wagon. They gently lifted the sheriff's lifeless body and laid it in another wagon, tying his gelding to the tailgate.

"Dat ol' man was tryin' to steal my mule!"

One of the freighters picked up the gun and noticed the badge. "My God! It's Sheriff Moore!" One wagon took the sheriff's body home, while the other two carried the Negro and led the mule to Centerville. The man who had come to Leon County as a ten year old, who had battled Indians and Mexicans, who had kept the peace for countless years, lay beaten to death by a murdering thief.

I rode out with the Centerville Sheriff to tell Mrs. Moore. When she saw the two of us riding up together, she knew. The tears came in a flood.

"He was such a good man, so good to me, and to the children."

The tears rolled down her face. She straightened her back. "He told me after you went with him to see Logan, that if anything happened to me, he wanted you to buy his half interest in the cattle and lease the land."

"Mrs. Moore, I'm so sorry. He was so good to me and my family, especially in all that trouble with my step-father, Lige. I don't know what we would have done without him. Yes ma'am, I'll buy the cattle and lease the land. I'll do anything else I can to help out."

My next stop was almost as difficult. The county sheriff had gone back to Centerville to try to deal with the trouble he knew would be coming. My job wasn't any easier. I had to tell Logan Morgan. I tied my horse on the porch rail. "Mrs. Morgan? May I come in? How is Mr. Morgan?"

"Aaron, you're always welcome here. He's sinking pretty fast. You look upset. What's wrong?"

"Ma'am, a colored man Sheriff Moore was trying to arrest beat him to death. I need to tell Logan."

"Oh, my Lord! Tanner was one of the finest men in Texas. It's gonna kill him, Aaron. That was his best friend in the world. I'll step in there with you." She wiped away her tears and led me to Logan's room.

Sunken yellowed eyes looked questioningly at me. A shriveled hand motioned weakly for me to come over.

"Ol' friend, you look rough. I'm here with bad news. Tanner Moore got killed by a thief this morning."

Tears trickled down his withered face. He began to cough until he turned blue. Finally catching his breath, he spoke in wheezing whispers. "He was the best friend I ever had. Came out here together in 1822." A fit of coughing seized his frail dying body. "Nothin' left here but ashes." A deep rumbling cough shook his whole body. He sighed and went limp. His eyes glazed over; his suffering was over. Ours was just about to begin.

———————————

The old church building had been swept out and cleaned for

the last services ever to be held there. The two coffins stood on saw horses at the front of the once fine building. People from all over the county packed into the sanctuary until they crowded along the walls and spilled out the door. A Baptist minister from Centerville led a respectable service. The widows, their children and grand-children filled the front pews, crying quietly. The preacher spoke of the changes and struggles these two had seen in their lifetimes. He told of the sacrifices they had made in the Indian Wars, the Texas Revolution, the Mexican War and the War Between the States. The county sheriff and the deputies from Marquez, Buffalo and Oakwood served as pallbearers and an honor guard for Sheriff Moore. Noah, Pecos, Shelby and I were the pallbearers for Mr. Morgan. They were buried in the small cemetery where their parents were buried south of the Camino Real.

I bought the cattle and leased the land. We helped both families load their belongings and watched them roll away. Mother lived in Limestone County now. Tanner and Logan had been the last of the original settlers and my last ties to the past except for her. There was land and livestock, but there was no human bond tying my heart to Leon County.

———————

The Leon County District Court had been replaced by a military court. A Yankee captain served as district attorney. He convened a grand jury of eleven Negroes and one carpetbagger. The white male population of Leon County was excluded from service by the Iron Clad Oath. The attorney didn't call the three teamsters who had seen the murder, or the man who owned the mule as witnesses. He let the sharecropper testify. He claimed the sheriff had been trying to steal his mule. When the lawman advanced on him with a gun, he struck him in the head with a single tree in self-defense. After deliberating only thirty minutes, the grand jurors returned a ruling of self-defense. The killer was released and the mule was returned to his rightful owner. The white members of the county, especially those who had been friends of Sheriff Moore, had packed the courthouse and the square around it. When the verdict was announced, the crowd fell into a stunned silence.

"First Platoon, attention! Forward march!"

"Second Platoon, attention! Forward march!"

"Third Platoon, ready, take aim. Hold your fire!" Orders were being shouted from the second floor gallery of the courthouse. Platoons of black troops advanced on the courthouse grounds with leveled bayonets from two different directions. Another platoon had their rifles aimed into the crowd from the gallery. A dozen heavily armed black state policemen escorted the jurors, district attorney, and the newly freed defendant down the courthouse steps and through the astonished crowd. We had just had our first experience with Reconstruction justice. It left a taste of ashes in my mouth.

———————

Tysoe rode up on a mule to the old store where we lived. Noah, Pecos and I met him on the porch. Shelby had ridden off earlier. "Massa Aaron, the Ku Klux is ridin' tonight. You best git yore sharecroppers where you kin take care of 'em."

"Tysoe, you stay here with Noah. Pick out a gun from the rack and make sure it's loaded. Keep the door barred. Come on, Pecos." We rode the hundred yards to the three sharecropper cabins that formed the three remaining sides of the old fort. The families appeared on their porches when we galloped up. "The Klan is ridin'. Get your families and whatever you can carry down to the store as fast as you can. If you got a gun, bring it loaded."

Pecos and I opened the stalls and turned our horses, mules and milk cows loose and drove them down into the thickets along the river. The trading post had been built in the days of Comanche raids. My father had built the roof of clay tile. There were rifle ports along each wall. The front door was reinforced two inch thick oak with heavy locking bars and hinges. The logs could burn, but would be difficult to ignite. It was the safest place we could be. Tysoe and the three sharecroppers were given shotguns. Pecos, Noah and I had our Henry repeating rifles and our Colt pistols. Extra guns were on a table in the middle of the room, including Noah's .50 caliber breech-loading Sharps rifle. We were as ready as we could be.

Flames flickered in the night air, as hooves pounded the dirt roads near Centerville. Thirty-three riders in white sheets and hoods galloped south away from the burning house of the district attorney. His dead body hung from a tree in front of the embers of his home. The ghostly riders thundered south to the murderer's cabin. Three black state policemen stepped from the door only to be gunned down where they stood. Four Klansmen entered the cabin and dragged the cursed man outside and placed a noose around his neck. He watched in horror as the door was nailed shut and the cabin burned with his wife and children inside. At that point, he was hanged to death and left swinging from an oak branch. The riders' blood was boiling. They galloped on to Navasota Crossing.

The white clad riders reined up in front of our old store on the Camino Real, spreading into a wide semi-circle. Their torches threw a threatening glare. A rough voice erupted from the hooded horsemen. "Six of you boys cover the back. Ain't none of these darkies getting' out of here alive. Aaron Turner, I figure you're in there with your brother and Pecos. We got no trouble with ol' Rebs like you. Send them darkies out now and we'll leave you alone." Gun barrels appeared from every gun port in the old store.

"You're right I'm in here with a lot of folks who can shoot straight. We got women and children in here, too. These are my share-croppers. They ain't done nothin' wrong. Just ride on!" I turned to Pecos. "Look at the spurs on the rider on the big bay."

"I'd recognize those spurs anywhere. That's Shelby, damn him!"

"You're a no good niggar-lover! Burn 'em out!" One of the riders tossed a burning coal oil lamp on the roof. I shot him dead. Pecos had fired simultaneously and killed their leader. They returned a heavy barrage of rifle and pistol rounds into the sturdy old cabin. Noah and Tysoe had fired at almost the same time we had, and two more were knocked dead out of their saddles. A Klansman tossed a torch on the front porch. I shot him through the chest before the torch landed. Seeing their loss of six men with no effect on the store, they wheeled their horses and rode straight to the sharecropper's cabins. In their rage, they burned the cabins, barns, corn cribs and outhouses. They pushed wagons into the fire and tossed in plows to burn their handles. Noah had all he could take. Using the flames which silhouetted the raiders, Noah aimed the deadly accurate Sharps to kill the Klansmen at long distance. Realizing their danger, they galloped off to the north along the river road.

A long night passed as we watched the dry log buildings burn to the ground. By daylight, the tile roofs collapsed into the hot coals that had been cabins. The flames licked upward into the still winter air. The sharecroppers had lost everything but their lives. We dared not leave the safety of the trading post for fear that the Klansmen still lurked in the darkness. The pounding of shod horse on the Camino Real about daylight got our attention. Guns bristled from every gun port only to see a company of Negro cavalry ride up with their white officers. A black sergeant rode up with a white flag on the end of his rifle. He saw the bodies of the dead Klansmen on the ground and the fresh bullet marks on the log walls. "Sergeant Hawkins, Fourth Cavalry, Company B. You folks need help?" I walked out on the porch carrying my Henry.

"We could have used help last night. Where were you?"

A voice behind me echoed from the door. "I'm comin' out, too, Massa Aaron." It was Tysoe cradling his twelve gauge. "Mornin' Sergeant. Y'all sho missed a good fight las' night. Mistah Turner put us all up here jes in case da Klan came. A whole mess of 'em showed up, and some of 'em didn't leave. They tried to burn us out, but we fought 'em off. Dey didn't hurt none of us, but burnt down all da cabins and outbuildin's. Dis man here saved our lives."

Slowly, the rest of the share croppers came out on the porch in tears. The Captain rode up. "Who's in charge here?"

"I guess I am, Captain." I handed the rifle to Tysoe and offered my hand to the officer. He looked at it like it was dirty and failed to shake my hand, or get down from his horse. This was an insult to me.

"Those Klansmen killed the district attorney, four state policemen, the accused man and his family. Looks like they came here to cause trouble. How did you know they were coming?"

"Tysoe told me the Klan was ridin'. Seemed like the thing to do."

"You people killed these Klansmen?"

"Yes, and one or two more over where the cabins used to be."

"From this far, I rather doubt it. Lieutenant, take a platoon up there and scout around."

When he returned the lieutenant grinned at me when he reported. "They burned everything that would burn. There are three dead Klansmen there and a dead horse. They've got holes in them the size of a man's fist."

Noah stepped out with the Sharps. "I shot those. You got a problem with that?"

"You men should have waited for the military or state police to take care of this."

"Mistah Captain, sah. If we had done dat we'd all be dead."

The captain stayed on his horse and had the hoods pulled off the dead Klansmen, including those retrieved from the burned out cabins. "Can you identify any of these men?"

Pecos, Noah and I looked at the faces and recognized all of them. Some were nothing but outlaws, but some were farmers, cattlemen and business owners. "Don't recognize any of them. Must be river trash from over on the Trinity." I didn't identify them for the retaliation I knew would come to their families.

"Which way did they leave?"

"North, up the river road."

"You Rebs best not cause us any trouble, or you'll wind up like these men here." He wheeled his company and took off at a slow trot up the river road.

———

We gave the sharecroppers an old wagon from the abandoned

blacksmith shop, two mules and some groceries. I wrote out a bill of sale on the wagon and mules so they wouldn't be accused of stealing them. They pointed the old wagon west and left at a trot. "Tysoe, do you think they know you were here?"

"I doan know, sah. Nobody saw me but dem soldiers. I got me a good place here. I'm ready to meet da Lord. I ain't goin' nowhere. I can ride around and check on da cattle on yo place and da sheriff's place. Nobody gonna pay much attention to one ol' darkie on a broke down mule. I bet dem Ku Klux doan come back here any time soon."

We looked through the smoldering ruins of what had once been a sturdy little fort. There was nothing left to salvage. We didn't bury the Klansmen. We laid them out along the road hoping their families would claim the bodies. It wouldn't be safe for us to spend any time here. Our days as residents of Leon County had come to an end. We gathered the horses and mules. We loaded everything in the two wagons that had been behind the store, one of which was our heavy trail wagon. The stink of ashes and death lingered in the air. It was sickening and I was ready to leave. We pointed the wagons and loose horses west on the Camino Real. We were moving west.

14

Moving on

WE DIDN'T SEE SHELBY AGAIN.
I guess he knew he was caught or ashamed. I never knew.
But there was a debt to pay, a score to settle. It would have
to wait, for we were in bad days. Negro troops were everywhere. They became bolder with their taunts and insults
as they realized that we couldn't strike back. The Ku Klux
Klan became more active and vicious. Those of us in the
middle were in a hard place.

There arose from the Radical Republicans a new
leader, Edmund J. Davis. He had been born in Florida,
and moved to Texas before the war. He was a staunch
Unionist, and now was the most radical of Republicans. He
had served as a Brigadier General in the Federal Cavalry
and was a friend and ally of President Grant. Davis had
used his influence to have Negro troops guarding the polls
in the fall election. His supporters infiltrated the election
boards across the state. With the Iron Clad Oath keeping
ninety percent of the white population from voting and the
active support of the military, he was swept into office in
November 1869. Radical Republicans gained enough seats

to control both houses of the legislature. Davis declared that the old Confederates of Texas were a conquered people. We were not conquered in spirit, for we remained "unreconstructed."

———————

We filed homestead claims on a section each for Mother, Noah and me along a creek that fed into Pecan Bayou where we had built the dugout and corral. We paid fifty cents an acre for surveying. The state allowed us to buy adjoining sections for fifty cents an acre as long as we paid for the surveying. We used some of our cattle money that had been resting in the Cattleman's Bank to buy and homestead six sections. We had a tract three miles long and two miles wide of some of the prettiest cattle country in Texas with the creek running the length of the property right down the middle.

Noah, Pecos and I went down to work on our claim awhile. We built wing fences leading into the corral, improved the dugout a little, and hand dug a well. Once the dirt settled, the water was sweet and clear.

Using our eight gentle oxen we caught mavericks in all directions. They remained yoked together until they seemed settled down and inclined to stay. We branded them AT on the left hip, plus the upside down T road brand for those we planned to market, then cut a half-moon notch in the top of both ears. There were plenty of cows of all ages, many with calves. We castrated the grown bulls and bull calves.

We brought four more half-blood Devon bulls to join the full-blooded bulls we had brought earlier. The big Devon bulls we had released the year before were all still on our range. They had wintered well. Many of the calves appeared to be half Devon. It would take a few years, but removing the longhorn bulls and adding the Devons would really upgrade the cattle. The crossbred calves were meatier and larger framed and quite a bit calmer than their long horned cousins. By fall we had one hundred and fifty pairs and over a hundred stags. We hoped they would survive and prosper in our absence.

The range was beautiful rolling prairie with motes of live oak trees. There were cottonwoods, elm and hackberry along the streams and draws with isolated patches of cedar. The native grasses were thick and grew in a beautiful patchwork of heights and subtly varying shades of green. There was switch grass and sprangle top that grew waist high in places. Blue and side oats grama was everywhere as was buffalo grass. In damp places, wheat grass grew that would be green in the cool months of late fall and early spring. For grazing cattle, it was a "Garden of Eden." I hated to leave.

———————

Christmas at Groesbeck with Mother was different. Although it was the building in which I had lived my whole life, I couldn't hear the Navasota River from my bedroom window. It wasn't surrounded by the fields my father had plowed or the pastures he had fenced. But home was where Momma lived. It would have to be enough for now.

I ran into Kelly Webb at Mexia. He had moved there in the past year. "Look what the cats drug up. Where you been hidin'?"

"Hey, you ol' toothless coot. We been catchin' cattle out west. Plannin' on puttin' together a herd for Kansas in the spring. You up for cookin' for us?"

"I wouldn't miss it. I wanna introduce my wife and kids. This is Lisa, she's from up near Sulphur Springs, my daughter Kelsey, the twins, Makayla and Makenzie, and my boy, Jake. We moved down here from Hunt County this winter and leased a little place."

"We got a boy named Jake that helps your Daddy with the cookin'. You get a little older, we'll take you, too."

"Heard you boys had some Klan trouble over in Leon County."

"Yeah. That's why we moved to Limestone County. They were pretty worked up; burned us out except the old store where we forted up."

"Where's that rascal Shelby? He dead yet?"

I looked away. "Ain't seen him in a while. He don't ride for me anymore."

"Never trusted him anyhow. Say, I met a fella from up near

Dallas. He's buyin' land and payin' in gold or silver. Now, he's a Yankee, but seems like a decent sort anyhow. You interested?"

"I'm always interested in hard money. I'll talk to Noah and Mother."

"We're gonna drive our Leon county cattle over to Waco in March, then gatherin' our stock out west. We hope to have everything in Waco to leave for Kansas around June 1. You're goin' ain't ya?"

"With a wife and three daughters, I'm always lookin' for somewhere to go."

———————

"Aaron, Leon County has been my home for almost fifty years, but there's nothin' left there but trouble. Our sharecroppers got run off and all our farm buildings got burned to the ground. The only friend we got left over there is old Tysoe. I'm all in favor of talking to this man."

"Kelly said he's from Missouri, named Smith. Has a reputation as a fair man for a Yankee. I'll see about talkin' to him."

Dallas had grown plenty since the last time I was there. Steamboats filled the Trinity and railroads were building in that direction. There were hotels, banks, taverns, churches, schools and houses sprawling into a town of a few thousand people. I found Mr. Smith at a modest hotel on the square across from the new courthouse. He was dressed like any farmer in bib overalls and rough brogans. "Mr. Smith?"

"Yes, I suppose you're Aaron Turner?"

"Yessir. Nice to meet you." We shook hands and sat down in two comfortable chairs in the lobby.

"I've seen your land in Leon County. Your letter said you'd consider selling it. I'm a Democrat. I don't hold with the current administration's policies. I fought for the Union, my brother fought for the south. We farm together now."

"I'm sure glad you're not a dang Republican. This tract of land has been in the family since my father got it as a Spanish land grant of a league and a labor. When Texas became part of Mexico, he refiled it, and the same for the Republic. I've got all the papers." I pulled out an ancient heavy canvas envelope. Inside was an oiled leather folder. Opening the folder, I carefully removed and unfolded the thick paper. It was written in Spanish and embossed with the seals of Spain and Mexico. There was a smaller paper written in brown ink with a hand drawn map and the seal of the Republic of Texas. I had a certificate showing all the taxes were current and an affidavit from the Leon County Clerk that there were no liens against the property.

Mr. Smith carefully looked at each page. "This is remarkable documentation. I have ridden over the property. The plowed ground looks fertile, and the pastures are in good condition. Unfortunately, all the farm buildings have been destroyed. I'm prepared to offer you two dollars an acre for the entire four thousand six hundred acres. I can pay half in gold at closing and give you a bank draft for the rest."

"Mr. Smith, that seems kinda cheap. We just gave fifty cents an acre for unsurveyed prairie land out west."

"You are quite right; it is cheap. Land values have dropped because of the very low price of cotton. Good cropland should be worth ten times the price of prairie, but currently that isn't the case. I can assure you it is a fair price for the times. Perhaps you would rather keep it until prices recover."

"No. We had already decided to sell it if we could get at least two dollars an acre. We want to hold out a quarter acre cemetery on the northeast corner of the property where my father is buried. Can we meet you at the Centerville courthouse a week from today?"

"Of course. Let me write it all down. I'll give you one hundred dollars in gold as earnest money now. We'll need to write a sale contract it to make it binding." We both signed it, and he counted out five double eagles.

The iron-rimmed buggy wheels cut silently into the soft mud of the Camino Real. Noah drove the buggy with mother. Pecos, Pink, Marcus and I rode behind them. We were heavily armed. Even Mother carried a double barreled shotgun. She wanted to see the old home place one more time. We left after midnight to get to Navasota Crossing by mid-morning. Pecos spurred ahead to check the crossing. No one stirred. He rode back and leaned over to talk to me. "They been back. They burned the store to the ground."

The river was low, so the buggy and horses hardly got wet. Mother gasped as she saw the remains of the store and burned out buildings. Noah circled the pile of debris where they had stood. There was nothing but cold ashes and stubs of chimneys. Cracked and broken tile filled the center of the charred remains that had been our trading post. "Momma, I got a bad feelin' that we better go check on Tysoe."

Nothing but ashes remained of his cabin and barn. "Aaron, Noah, come over here. Pink would you and Marcus stay there with your mother?" What remained of Tysoe hung from an oak tree. The body dangled from a noose in an oak tree. The flesh had fallen from the bones, but the grizzled gray hair remained above the empty eye sockets.

"Klansmen! This ol' man never hurt anybody." We cut the rope and lowered what remained of his body to the ground. We buried him right there in a shallow grave. Noah set up a large stone at the head of the grave.

Mother came walking up. "Boys, it's only fitting we pray over him. Noah, would you mind?" He complied with a simple prayer committing our friend to the Lord's keeping. Sadly, we moved on, making a stop at the small cemetery where my father was buried, as well as some children who had died before I was born. We spent a few minutes gathering up fallen branches. "Aaron, I loved your father with all my heart, but please don't bury me in Leon County. It is a place of sad, bitter memories now."

We hurried along the Centerville road, reaching the court-house at the appointed time. Mr. Smith was waiting. We made introductions all around and entered the courthouse together. We signed the deeds Mr. Smith had prepared. He paid us the gold coin he had promised and handed us a bank draft for the rest. I walked across the street and sent a telegram to my bank in Waco. Within half an hour, they confirmed the draft was good. Noah, Mother and I signed the deed and the land purchased with blood, sweat and tears passed out of our family forever. Our days as residents of Leon County were over. As my family had done for four generations, we looked west for a better life.

———————

Mr. Smith had agreed to give us time to remove our cattle. We pushed the Moore and Morgan herd in with our main herd. These were all good quality crossbred cattle. We would separate the cows and heifers to move to our place on Pecan Bayou. The barren cows and steers would be held at Captain Tyus' ranch until we were ready to head for Abilene. Noah rode with us this time. It was good to spend time with him again. I would soon be twenty and he was twenty-two, but the war had aged us. With quick work, we combined the herds and headed west. We drove the cattle across the Navasota River. I realized at the time that it was unlikely I would have a reason to return. Pecos rode up. "Can you feel it, Aaron? This place that had always been so good is full of bad spirits now. It's right we're leavin'."

"It's not just you, Injun boy; I feel it, too. The sooner we get out of here the better." We had gathered the horses and swept the thickets near the ranch to gather up a few strays. The hogs and chickens were turned loose to their own devices. We left nothing behind but memories. In five days, we reached the Captain's place.

"Cap, it's good to see ya! We've been to hell and back since the last time we talked." I brought him up to date on all that had happened.

"Aaron, you did the right thing, and it cost you. Moving out of Leon County was the only choice you had. Is your mother alright with all this?"

"Yessir. She's pretty tough, but she didn't want any part of Leon County after all this. I wish you could see our place out west. It's beautiful. We're leavin' in the mornin'."

"If you don't mind, I'll go with you."

———————

"King Cotton" had come to Texas because the Yankee, Eli

Whitney, had invented the cotton gin. Now "King Cotton" was on his death bed. The price of cotton was too low to cover the cost of growing it. Land prices dropped with the price of cotton. The old planter class in Texas was gone, never to return. Northern mills reaped enormous profits off the backs of small farmers and sharecroppers from the South. Texas' economic woes only deepened. Kiowa raids continued to make life miserable for Texans along the Red River. Satanta and his followers terrorized isolated farms, killing settlers and stealing livestock. The Comanche raided aggressively all along the western frontier. The new line of forts was kept busy. To venture up on the plains was to risk death.

––––––––––

The real plague on Texas continued to be southern scalawags, northern carpetbaggers, Yankee officers and their Negro troops. The greatest plague was the Radical Republicans and their leader, Governor Edmund J. Davis.

The twelfth Texas legislature was seated. The thirty members of the Senate included seventeen Radical Republicans, of which two were Negroes, seven Conservative Republicans and six Democrats. The ninety members of the House seated fifty Radical Republicans, including eleven Negroes, nineteen Conservative Republicans and twenty-one Democrats. They quickly ratified the Fourteenth and Fifteenth Amendments.

Governor Davis had an agenda. He wanted the next governor's election delayed until after 1872. Davis pushed for a Militia Bill. It would give the Governor the authority to declare martial law in any political subdivision of the state at any time. All men in the jurisdiction between eighteen and forty-five would be forced to join the militia under the command of the Governor or his representative, then taxed to pay for the cost of martial law. He asked for the establishment of a special State Police force with state-wide jurisdiction. This police force would be directly answerable only to the Governor. A special Printing Bill would allow the state to pay "approved publishers" for printing all official news. The most powerful new law would give the governor the right to appoint or remove any official in the state of Texas from the Supreme Court to the county surveyor. The political consequences would be immense.

All of the Democrats and some of the Conservative Republicans refused to support the Davis agenda. Governor Davis had them arrested. Finally, it was noticed that there were not enough members present to have a quorum. He had four members brought to the capital building in chains and under guard to achieve the required number. The entire legislative package passed.

Newspapers that expressed displeasure with the Governor were visited by the state police. Legislators who opposed Davis received special attention from his personal police force.

I had thought things were bad in Texas before now, but it was nothing compared to what had befallen our poor "conquered people." The beast had emerged and truly evil days were upon us. The people cried out for justice and found fraud. They cried out for freedom and found brutal oppression. The harvest of hatred was being reaped. The grapes of wrath were yielding a bitter wine.

15

Gathering on Pecan Bayou

WE HAD DRIVEN ALL THE stock we owned out of Leon County to McLennan County. We sorted off those cattle destined for Abilene and left them at the Captain's ranch. We were moving the breeding stock to our ranch on Pecan Bayou. We would retrieve more market cattle there and bring them back before starting up the Chisholm Trail. As we prepared to leave for the western frontier, a wagon pulled onto the road led by Captain Tyus on horseback. A familiar voice boomed from the seat of the wagon. "You're not leavin' without the cook are ya?"

"Kelly Webb! We weren't expectin' you until we leave for Kansas."

"I didn't want to see you bein' called no greasy sack outfit without a good cook and wagon. I went by and got your wagon fixed up and supplied for the trip out to Pecan Bayou. The truth is, with a wife and three daughters at home, I was huntin' somewhere to go."

We set out pushing about two hundred and fifty head of quality breeding stock. The Brazos River was low and the cattle splashed across, hardly getting their bellies wet. As spring was coming on, the grass along the way became green enough for fresh grazing. We didn't push the cows, but let them take their time and fill up every day. There were plenty of deer with fawns in the brush and turkey everywhere. The arrival of spring was a good tonic after a hard winter.

The water of Pecan Bayou was cold and clear. We could see fish swimming around the rocks in the stream bed. A herd of buffalo rolled and grunted in a sandy patch of ground trying to remove the faded reddish hair of winter. Flocks of geese and sandhill cranes flew north so high in the crystal clear sky they were easier to hear than to see.

We followed the north fork of Pecan Bayou. Wild cattle with speckled calves, yearlings with sharp short horns and old moss back bulls grazed the meadows. Soon our dugout and pens came into view. The pastures spread out on either side of the creek. We drove the cattle to drink and they soon settled in to graze. Hearing strange cattle was a lure the other cattle couldn't resist. Within an hour they came sniffing out of the brush and socializing with their gentle crossbred counterparts. Scattered among the longhorns were dark red and red speckled calves from our Devon bulls.

Kelly kept us in biscuits, bacon and beans. Captain Tyus was a better officer and lawyer than he was a cowhand. He couldn't rope a stump if he was standing still, but he knew his way around a horse and was good help herding and working the cattle. We sorted the breeding cattle from the market herd. Those cattle destined for Kansas had already been road branded with the upside down T on their left ribs. We made a last sweep around the perimeter and drove in a few strays.

"Noah, Pecos. We got this job whipped. Let's head 'em to Waco and on to Abilene."

"I think I'm gonna go with ya, little brother."

"I didn't think you liked cow work that much."

"I don't. But I enjoy spendin' time with you, knothead."

"How 'bout it, Cap? Wanna go up the trail?"

"No thank you! This has been plenty of fun, but I'm too old to drive cattle to Kansas."

"Biscuit's too old, but he's goin' anyway. He's our secret weapon against wolves. We leave a pot of his grub out ever night and find a few of 'em dead ever mornin'."

"I hadn't seen you turn any down, Pecos. Reckon you're too darn mean to poison."

"Ah, Biscuit, don't go puttin' salt in the coffee, we're just rawhidin' ya."

———

Our cattle bawled and milled around as they mixed with Captain Tyus' cattle. We had six hundred and fifty head, and the Captain had three hundred and fifty of his own cattle. The Dawsons rode in with two hundred head. Matt had grown to six feet tall and had filled out a good bit. He sure wasn't the twig that had gone to Sedalia with us in '66. Jake had shot up to five foot nine and was all arms and legs. "Hey, Michael, Matt and Jake! Good to see ya! You must be feedin' those boys good!"

"We gotta sell some cattle to keep 'em in clothes and groceries."

The Shepards showed up with Kyle, who looked like a grown man. They brought fifty head of good cattle.

Finally, Luke and Levi Carter came in pushing sixty head of home raised steers. "Start the party, the Carter boys are here!" Levi crowed. He looked nearly grown, and Luke sure wasn't the little drowned rat Shelby pulled out of the river four years ago.

Pecos and Matt threw shoes on all the horses and mules. Noah rechecked the wagon, but found that Kelly had pretty much taken care of things. Kelly picked up his draft horse he had left at the Captain's place and rode with Jake into Waco to get supplies. "Aaron, Jake is too good a cowhand to waste helpin' me cook. The Captain has got a kid here named Zach Barton, about twelve, to help me. He's a good hand with horses, too."

Kelly found the boy and brought him to meet me. "Howdy, Slim. You know anything about horses?"

"Reckon I know how to keep 'em from runnin' off at night. I don't fall off very often. I know where the oats go in and the apples come out."He grinned mischievously.

"How about cookin'?"

"Ten tablespoons of Arbuckle's coffee to boilin' water; let 'er simmer, and then add an egg shell to settle the grounds. Serve it hot, black and strong."

"Kelly, what do ya say?"

"He brought three good horses, a bedroll and a war bag. He's drivin' fifteen head of his own cattle. He'll do."

"Pay is twenty-five dollars and found."

"Mr. Turner, I'm big enough to be worth thirty dollars a month. I'm a hard worker."

"Good grief, Zach. If you work as good as you talk, you'll get thirty."

"Kelly, Cap says you brought twenty head when you came down from Mexia. Any of 'em stolen?"

"Not that anybody around here knows about." He laughed.

"Cap, that puts us at one thousand three hundred and forty-five head; that's the biggest herd we've sent up the trail yet. And it's a good time to be out of Texas for a while."

16

May 13, 1870, McLennan County, Texas

On the Chisholm Trail Again

"HUP MULES! HUP!" THE WHIP cracked over the broad backs of our best bay mules. The wagon lurched forward on to the road. Zach slapped his rope against his chaps to start the horses. Most of them had been up the trail before, and this was nothing new. They fell in behind the wagon.

"Start 'em up, Pecos!" He stood in the stirrups and waved his hat to the other drovers. The cattle got up rear end first, stretched, and moved lazily behind the horses. Pecos was still segundo. Matt had earned the place of honor on the right point previously held by Shelby. The Carter boys moved up to flank, so Jake and Kyle rotated the dusty duty at drag with them. I took Noah on point with me. I didn't need him up there; I just wanted to spend time with him. We had been close before the war, but after spending those three years together, we were best friends for life.

The first night on the trail Kyle asked about Shelby. "Aaron, what happened to Shelby? Why ain't he ridin' with us this year?"

"Yeah. I sure liked him. He saved my life on the Arkansas." Luke asked. I looked at Noah and Pecos not knowing what to say. Kelly just shrugged.

"Boys, Shelby has ridden with us for five years. He saved you from drownin', and he saved Pecos' bacon one time. He got us out of that jackpot with the James gang up on the Cherokee Strip. But Shelby's got a bad side. He's runnin' with some pretty bad men. I'm not gonna tell ya the details. You be careful if he shows up. That bad side has taken hold of him. He's dangerous. Me, Noah and Pecos got to settle some things with him." They sat there puzzled and quiet. Pecos pitched his coffee in the fire and walked off. When we did see Shelby again, it wasn't gonna be good.

We didn't stop in Fort Worth, but headed on to the Red River. Kelly talked Noah into driving the wagon for him for a bit. He saddled up his huge horse and rode into town to buy more tobacco. He gummed that stuff like a rat eats cheese.

When we got to Red River Station, they told us that Satanta and about one hundred and fifty warriors were raiding all up and down the river. There was a large band of outlaws riding in the same area. Levi leaned over. "Wouldn't it be good if the outlaws got in a big fight with the Kiowa and wiped each other out?" I had to admit I liked the idea.

We crossed the Red without difficulty and camped a few miles north of the river. Everyone was on edge that night. We still left just two men on guard with the herd, but two more were awake at camp until they were off shift. Everyone slept with one or more loaded guns. We had Zach picket and hobble the remuda.

———————

Distant gunfire shattered the stillness of the humid night air. From the sound of it, there were lots of guns two or three miles away. "Put out that fire! Kelly, you use the wagon for cover and have the boys drag up logs and rocks to make a semi-circle backin' up to the wagon. Load every gun you got. Matt, I'm leavin' you and Kelly in charge here. Pecos, you and Noah grab your night horses and come now."

We rode at a fast trot down the trail toward the Red River. The gunfire suddenly increased, then died away to sporadic shooting. Whoever was fighting, it was over and they were shooting the survivors. A red glow appeared just to the side of the trail ahead. Gun smoke mixed with wood smoke drifted on the light breeze. We eased a little farther ahead, and then hid at the side of the trail. We dismounted and held our hands over our horses' noses. One nicker could reveal our presence. Hoof beats struck the earth heading west along the river. We waited in silence. No sound came from the site of the fight. Once the fire had burned down to embers we led our horses to the edge of the timber east of the trail. The faint moonlight showed a smoldering wagon, several dead horses and many bodies scattered on the ground.

Tying his horse, Pecos eased across the trail to see what had happened. He silently surveyed the scene, keeping a low profile. He motioned for us to join him. In a whisper he explained what he knew. "Kiowa attacked a party of white men. There's sixteen bodies, maybe more. Looks like they stole most of the horses then killed and scalped all the men."

A gurgling quiet voice near us pleaded in the darkness. "Help me." We covered Pecos with our rifles as he crawled forward.

"Good Lord, its Shelby!" We scrambled over to see a grotesque sight. Shelby had an arrow through his throat and three in his chest. A large patch of scalp was missing down to the sickening white of his skull.

I got a grip on myself. "Are you Shelby?"

"Yes."

"This is Aaron Turner. I got Noah and Pecos here with me. You're in a bad way."

"Dying. Never thought I'd see ya again." He stopped to spit out the blood that was filling his mouth. "I was with the Klan the night we attacked your place and burned you out." He paused for breath. "I was mad as hell about that trial. I don't regret hangin' that Yankee lawyer or that murderin' darkie, but I'm mighty sorry about what we done to you." He gasped and coughed, spraying blood on all of us. "I done plenty of bad things in my life. That was one of the worst, turnin' on my true friends. I know I'm headin' straight to hell, but I want to ask you not to hate me for what I done. Can you forgive me?"

Pecos spoke first. "We forgive ya. We don't hate you, either. You just took a wrong turn."

Noah and I nodded agreement. "I got to ask you if you was in on killin' ol' Tysoe."

"Yes." He coughed hard and his eyes rolled back in his head. The bleeding in his neck slowed to ooze.

I laid my hand on his chest. "He's gone. We can't just leave him here."

"Why the hell not?" Pecos demanded.

"You said you forgave him."

"I said it to ease a dying man. But I hate him for what he did and I'm glad he's dead. It saved me from killin' him."

"Aaron, I'm with Pecos. We don't owe him nothin'. He killed one of the kindest ol' men I knew. I'm leavin' him here for the coyotes and crows."

Pecos kicked some dirt on the dead body. "That's good enough. Let's go."

———————

"Any trouble, Matt?"

"Nothin'. I'm sure glad you're back. What's the story?"

"Levi got his wish. A big band of Kiowa caught up with that outlaw gang. The outlaws are all dead as far as I can tell. Couldn't tell how many Kiowa they got 'cause they carried 'em off when they left. They got the horses and burned the wagon."

Kelly eyed us suspiciously. "That don't explain how all three of ya got blood splattered on your clothes and faces."

"Shelby was one of 'em. He wasn't quite dead when we found him, but he didn't last long. We didn't do anythin' to help him out of this world, if that's what you're thinkin'. That's all I got to say about it. The Kiowa are still around. I suspect Shelby's bunch hurt 'em good. It looks like there is way too many of them for us to handle. We gotta hope they don't catch up to us. No fire. No talkin' above a whisper.

We're havin' water, hard tack and jerky for breakfast, then push up the trail fast and hard."

"We left as soon as it was light enough to see. There was no way to hide a herd of cattle and the way we were going would be obvious. Noah and I split up and scouted for signs of trouble ahead. We pushed the cattle hard that day, not letting them graze their way up the trail, but moving at a fast walk to a trot. This would burn a little of the tallow off them, but it was better than losing our hair. We pushed on until just dark. We had covered eighteen miles that day. The cattle grazed for an hour in the twilight, then bedded down worn out. They sure weren't likely to stampede tonight. The horses were picketed and hobbled again. Our camp was on a small hill with a good view in every direction. We made a small barricade of whatever we had, including saddles, logs and crates. We kept our guns at our sides all night, and made do with no fire and cold food.

"Aaron, you and Pecos remember when we were stationed on Billy Goat Hill at Chattanooga?"

"Yeah. Ol' Sherman tried hard, but he couldn't get us off the hill. That's where we put the squirrel in Taylor's bedroll and it bit him right on the nose." We laughed for a minute. "I remember Pickett's Mill, too. I'll never forget that day as long as I live."

Pecos broke in, "At least the Yankees didn't try to scalp us!" We laughed in spite of the nervous tension that was building as we waited through the long night for a Kiowa attack that never came.

We drove the cattle a hard fifteen miles the next day, past one good pasture and on to the next. None of us had slept much the last two nights, and two hard days on the trail was taking a toll. We had almost thirty-five miles between us and the site of the massacre. Noah scouted ahead and I took the back trail. No sign, no smoke. Nothing. We didn't fort up that night, but kept two men awake at all times. The cattle were so tired they weren't going anywhere.

By the next day we dropped back to a normal pace, letting the cattle take their time, grazing along the way. We still made a respectable twelve miles. We turned the cattle in on a lush bed ground and enjoyed watching them fill up on good grass and water. Kelly and

Zach fixed bacon, beans, biscuits and gravy along with cane sorghum and lots of coffee. It was just what we needed.

———————

We drove the herd across the Wichita River at Rock Creek Crossing and made it to the Dover Stage Station in a few days. Kelly bought a few things, including some fresh vegetables. There was a stale newspaper from Fort Smith someone had left at the tavern. "Noah, Governor Davis got mad at Senator Hamilton for speaking out against him. He had the Texas Supreme Court declare his election invalid. He tried to have General Reynolds put in Hamilton's place, but when Reynolds got to Washington, the Senate refused to seat him and backed Hamilton. Went all the way to the United States Supreme Court; they ruled in favor of Hamilton. Bet that poked ol' Davis in the eye!" We all laughed as we considered Davis the world's largest pole cat.

Kelly fixed us sweet corn roasted in the shuck, squash boiled with a little onion and butter, fried chicken, biscuits and gravy. I didn't think I could eat another bite until he brought out a huge cobbler made with wild plums. "Biscuit, you outdid yourself this time." Pecos said as he patted his swollen stomach.

"Just you wait for breakfast if you liked that. Zach, don't tell 'em. It's a surprise."

We awoke to this aroma of coffee, but something tantalizing was in the air. Kyle wandered over for a look in the big skillet. "Boys, he's frying real ham and eggs!"

"And we got biscuits, honey, wild plum jelly and fresh butter." Zach beamed. "Plus a gallon of fresh milk to drink or put in your coffee."

"Ol' Biscuit's just showing off, ain't he Pecos."

Jake popped off, "It sure beats ersters, don't it Levi!"

"I wish y'all would shut up about that."

"Yeah, and it was my hat he puked in!" Luke complained.

We made it to one of the most beautiful places along the whole Chisholm Trail, Buffalo Springs in the edge of the Cherokee Strip. This was also the place we memorialized because of the feast Kelly had fixed for us two years ago. About supper time, an ancient Indian rode up on a young gray mule.

"John Walking Bear, we all figured you was dead."

"I ain't dead yet. Where's that fat, bald-headed, toothless ten foot tall sorry excuse for a cook?"

Kelly poked his head around the wagon. "John, I thought you was dead. Where's your ol' mule?"

"He died. I had to get me a new one. I miss that ol' mule; he was kinda stringy eatin'."

"You ate your own mule, you crazy ol' hoot owl?"

"You want me to eat one of yours instead, white man?" We all laughed. Those of us who had been in the war had eaten enough horse and mule to last us for a lifetime. We swapped stories, lies and tall tales way up in the night. As usual, John ate enough for three men.

We paid our pasture fees the next morning and got a receipt from John. "You boys had any more outlaw trouble? I didn't see Shelby around."

"Shelby got killed in a Kiowa raid down on the Red River. He had gone as bad as three day-old fish."

————

The trip across the Arkansas was quiet. The river was low and crossing was easy. The riverboats wouldn't be able to make it up to Bent's Fort until there was a big rise on the river. We cut on up across Kansas. There was a small town named Caldwell just inside the state line where they were building cattle shipping pens. I stopped to talk to the foreman. "Y'all expectin' the railroad in here soon?"

"Not soon enough to suit me, but the Atchison-Topeka-Santa Fe is buildin' a line down here just for cattle. Seems some of the folks in Abilene is gittin' kinda tired of Texas cowboys."

"This would knock three weeks off the trip. Maybe we'll be doin' some business here on the next drive."

The cattle slowly plodded on toward Abilene. They had fallen into their routine. I believe they would have kept walking right on to Canada. They had fattened nicely along the way and were by anyone's standards prime beef. On August 3, 1871, we bedded the herd down on the south bank of the Solomon River across from Abilene. It was obvious we were the first herd of the season. Joseph McCoy came out to meet us. The Deputy United States Marshall came with him. "Good to see you, Aaron. This is the best looking herd you've brought up the trail. I'd guess two-thirds of them are crosses. They're good and fat, too.

"Howdy, Mr. McCoy. Glad you like 'em. They're good stock. What are they bringin'?"

"You Texans like to get right down to business. The price is off some. They'll bring twenty-five dollars a head, plus a two dollar bonus for being the first herd."

"Is anybody offerin' more? I sure liked forty a head better."

"No. I always try to give you my best price."

"It's a deal. Sheriff Webb, you the welcomin' committee from the Ladies' Temperance Society?"

The boys all snickered while he turned red in the face. "It's Marshall Webb. I think you boys kept me busy while your friend got away. There's a three hundred dollar bounty on him."

"Not any more there ain't. He's dead as a doorknob down on the Red River. Collected himself a chest full of Kiowa arrows and lost his hair."

"You tellin' the truth, Turner?"

"John Law, I may be a lot of things, but I ain't no liar. Me, Noah and Pecos got there before he died. If it makes you feel any better, he said he was real sorry for all the bad things he done."

"If you're claimin' the reward, you gotta sign some affidavits."

"Shelby used to be a friend of mine until he got to runnin' with the Klan, burned down my farm and turned outlaw. You got an orphanage here?"

"Well, yes. Why?"

"I'll sign those papers if Mr. McCoy sees that the money goes to the orphans. It's blood money. I ain't touchin' it, but at least Shelby would do somethin' good when he died."

———————

Our count came out right and we made a stop at the bank. Zach had lived up to the thirty dollars a month he had wanted. Matt had moved up into Shelby's old job, so was drawing thirty-five a month. Noah asked to talk to me before we left the bank. "Aaron, you usually give me my share in a bank draft. I need it in coin this time."

"Why? Don't you trust banks anymore?"

"No. I made this trip on purpose. I ain't goin' back to Texas. I'm buyin' wagons and mules, and hirin' men to get into the buffalo hide business up on the Republican River." You could have knocked me over with a feather.

"What! You never said a word about it. What am I supposed to tell Momma?"

"I'll be back at some point. After that deal with the Klan I lost my taste for Texas. I want to get away from all that. I figure this will get me about as far away as anything. Tell Momma I'll be back with my hair on my head and sacks full of money."

"Noah, that's rough, dangerous work. Hide hunters are some of the roughest fellas I ever seen."

"Maybe it won't rub off on me. When I figure out where I'll be based, I'll write or telegraph you. If somethin' happens to me, my share of the cattle and ranch goes to you."

"You better be darn sure to come home and claim your share!"

We all spent some of our money on clothes, new hats and presents to take home. Kelly and Zach restocked the wagon. Kelly bought out nearly the whole stock of tobacco in one store. "A fella cain't never have too much."

We all took advantage of the Chinese bathhouse and laundry, courtesy of Mr. McCoy. It sure felt good to be clean again. Those little wash-ups in creeks helped, but not like a full bath, shampoo, shave and a haircut. I looked like a new double eagle. We had our customary fancy dinner in Abilene, but to be honest, I preferred Ol' Biscuits' cooking.

We camped across the river to get an early start back to Texas. Pecos, Noah and I talked most of the night. We relived some of our times together during the war and the hard times since then. I told Noah he was the only full-blooded brother I had, and he dang sure better come home.

In the morning we headed south while Noah waved his hat at us until we couldn't see him anymore. Pecos was a friend, a very good friend, but Noah was my brother and my best friend in the world. It was hard to think of him being gone a year or two. It was unthinkable that he might not come home at all.

Levi always had a mischievous streak. One night just north of the Arkansas, he put a grass snake in Luke's bedroll. Luke gave all of us a pretty good show. A few days passed quietly without a sign of revenge. Then one night, Luke borrowed Kelly's shovel and half filled Levi's boots with fresh horse manure. When Biscuit hollered for breakfast, Levi gave us a pretty good show, too. Luke sure was proud of himself.

A couple of herds met us on the trail. We swapped news but didn't stay to socialize. We were headed home. When we came to the place where Shelby had died, we spent a few minutes looking around. There were scattered bones littering the ground, plus pieces of boots and clothes. Jake spotted something shiny and climbed down to investigate. It was Shelby's fancy spurs. "What should I do with these?"

"You ain't got any fancy spurs. I reckon Shelby would be glad for you to have them. He sure won't need 'em where he is."

"You don't reckon they're jinxed or nothin'?"

"The only thing wrong with them spurs was the fella wearin' 'em."

17

Hell on the Trail to Caldwell

THERE WAS A SICKNESS OVER the land. Not a sickness of the body, but of the soul. The war had been over for six years. The sounds of muskets and echoes of cannon were fading into memory. But the evil fruits borne on the bitter tree of war continued to poison the South. We could not vote. We could not hold office. We could not serve on a jury. The basic freedoms of Americans were denied to us. Those who sought profit and power from these evil times grew fat and arrogant.

Before Davis and the Radical Republicans had ascended to power, state property taxes had stood at fifteen cents per hundred dollars of assessed value. Now the tax rate stood at two dollars and seventy-eight cents. To make matters much worse, the Davis appointed tax assessors arbitrarily set the value of a particularly desirable piece of property much higher than the market value. The land owner could appeal to the Davis appointed Negro tax appraisal board. If they refused to lower the appraised value, the owner could appeal to the Davis appointed State District Court. The jury would be composed of Negroes and carpetbaggers. If they denied the request, it could be appealed to the Davis appointed Supreme Court. In the end, the land was auctioned on the courthouse steps for pennies on the dollar. Many choice properties were stolen from ex-Confederates by the Davis regime.

Anger against Davis, the Radical Republicans, the State Police and Negroes in general was rapidly rising. The elected men who were not Davis supporters grew sick of the behavior of "the hogs at the trough." They had seen enough. A coalition slowly began to form between the Conservative Republicans, the Democrats, and the disenfranchised masses of Texans. Something had to change.

"Come on Speck, move your bony rear! Keep that lineback in the herd, boys. That mulberry is headed to Kansas." The dust rose as we sorted out our market cattle. They were branded with the upside down T road brand and treated for ticks. Our Shorthorn cross cows had done well when bred back to the Devon bulls. We had lots of red and red roan long yearling steers that were big enough to market.

Pecos tied on to an old barren longhorn cow that had attached herself to the herd. She had horns at least six feet across. She was an orejano, a cow with unnotched ears. Her black and red brindle hide had no brand, a true maverick. The old cow charged straight at Pecos and his horse. He spurred to yank the slack out of the rawhide rope and trip the cow, but she was gaining on him. Matt and Jake jumped in to help. Matt threw a perfect loop that settled over her wide horns and pulled tight. Jake, no longer a skinny cook's helper, caught both her back feet with his first try. When his stout horse jerked the slack out of the rope, she went down hard. "Thanks, boys! Ol' 'Sugar Britches' just about got me. Let's slap a brand on her."

Zach came running up with a red hot iron. With two strokes, she was branded. He used his pocket knife to notch her big old ears. He eased the two ropes off her horns while her back feet were still tied.

"Just loosen that back rope and I'll shake it off. You run for it. If she tries to get ya, I'll jerk her down." Jake promised.

Newly named Sugar Britches sensed her feet were loose with

a kick. She raised her broad bony rump off the ground while Zach was still trotting toward the fire. Sugar Britches spotted him and let out an earth-shattering bellow. She bore down on him as fast as her ancient frame could travel. Kyle saw the danger and galloped in, grabbing Zach by the belt and dragging him out of the way. She turned her attention to the cook wagon. For a fat man, Kelly ran like a racehorse. She used her horns to thrash his pots and pans, scattering cast iron and flour in every direction. Levi shook out a loop and charged after the angry old cow. He caught her right hind foot. It was enough to throw her off balance. Luke joined in the chase. His loop missed her horns, but by pure luck, snagged both front feet. As they spurred their horses in opposite directions, she again hit the ground hard.

I rode up leading our largest ox and a heavy yoke. It took three of us, but we managed to yoke the wild cow to the gentle ox. As she got up, the ox used her great size and strength to drag her new friend anywhere she wanted to go.

————

Down Pecan Bayou, along the Colorado, across the Brazos and up the river road to Waco, we pushed a few more than six hundred good cattle. Captain Tyus was expecting us. He had four hundred of his own trail-ready cattle. Zach Barton had left ten head of his own cattle at the Captain's place. The Shepards had left sixty head there before Kyle had ridden out west with us. The Dawsons had brought in two hundred head, and the Carter boys added another seventy. Kelly had contributed thirty-five of the oddest assortment of cattle I ever saw. There were dairy cross steers, longhorns, worn out oxen, English-cross cattle of good breeding with several different brands and ear notches, but all recently branded with the upside down T. "Biscuit, how did you get such an odd collection of cows?"

"Tradin' work for cows. Somebody would have me cook for a gatherin', I'd take half my pay in cash and half in odds and ends of cattle. Most of them were only priced at two or three dollars. I think we can get twenty five for them at Caldwell. They usually give me some of the sorry ones, but I put 'em on grass and they look a little better. How many we got?"

"Right close to fourteen hundred head. Mr. McCoy said in his telegram that the railroad ought to be finished to Caldwell by the middle of July, just in time for us. He said he'd have an agent there. If not, we'll push on to Abilene."

Unyoked from her constant companion, Sugar Britches had a whole new outlook on life. She shouldered her way to the head of the herd and challenged any animal that tried to pass her. Zach and Kelly were keenly aware she was behind them, and made sure she didn't climb into their back pockets.

The trail to the Red River was peaceful. These cattle, being largely crosses, were the calmest we had ever driven. We checked for news at the trading post at Red River Station before crossing the Red River into the Nations.

"Them Kiowa took care of the outlaw problem around here last summer. Folks claim that campground is haunted. Won't nobody stay there for nothin'. Ol' Chief Satanta is still up to his tricks. You better make sure you got plenty of cartridges for them Henry rifles and powder and shot for the Colts. We got plenty of caps, too."

"Thanks. We're pretty well fixed. Give me a couple dollars worth of tobacco for my cook. He gets grouchy if he runs out."

The swirling red water was only neck deep on the cattle; they didn't have to swim. We passed the site of the massacre and kept riding. A few scattered, bleaching bones showed through the grass. When we bedded the cattle, it was two men with the herd, plus every hand slept fully armed.

The wind rose during the night from the south. Sheet lightning flashed within the clouds. Thunder rolled in the banked black and green thunderheads. "Everybody up! Kelly, saddle that big horse, this looks bad."

Yellow-green flickers of foxfire glowed on the tips of the nervous cows' horns. They shifted anxiously watching the strange light and listening to the unfamiliar hum. A moaning sound like a dying man was carried on the humid south wind. As the storm drew closer and the wind rose, so did the eerie sound. The unearthly groan reached a pitch that made the hair stand up on my neck. The foxfire danced down the backs and tails of the cattle and appeared on the astonished cowboys and riders. A blinding flash of lightning split open the heavens, instantly followed by an explosion of thunder that shook the earth down to its foundations. The cattle bolted straight north away from the lightning, away from the wind, away from the evil sound of death. They ran like the hounds of hell were on their heels. Their pounding hooves shook the ground. Flashes of lightning showed they were still together with Sugar Britches in the lead. Rain came in sheets from the south, the drops fat and cold, mixed with marble-sized hail.

Pecos got to his place at left point, followed by half the crew. They tried to keep the cattle on the wide trail. Matt did the same on the right point. I raced ahead and found a good place to turn them east into a large prairie. The cattle were already flagging some, slowing with each passing minute. Soon, they were down to a weary trot. The pasture loomed in the darkness on the right, visible in the lightning flashes.

Pecos saw the spot and had the men put a little pressure on the herd from the left side. At the same time, Matt and his drovers dropped back on the right. Sugar Britches saw the prairie open up ahead of her and veered off the trail into the tall wet grass. The others followed and made a wide, slow circle around the prairie before gradually stopping to graze. Within half an hour, the last of them eased wearily down onto the soggy ground.

"Good job, boys. Close as I can tell, they ran seven miles. Kyle, come with me to check the back trail. Kelly, you and Zach ride to the wagon. Get it up here and get some coffee goin'!"

Kyle found two steers that had broken legs. I rode over and slit their throats to stop their suffering. Kyle helped me butcher out the back meat and the hind quarters. At least we would enjoy some fresh meat. Pecos came loping up. "We can't find Levi. He was at the back of the right flank."

My stomach tightened. "Come on, let's go." The three of us

spread out along the right side of the trail. About a mile back down the trail Kyle saw Levi's horse.

"Aaron, it looks like he broke his neck. I pulled Levi's saddle off his horse. He must be close."

Pecos found his hat. Twenty feet away Levi lay crumpled on the ground. I reached for his neck. He had a pulse, but his left arm was badly broken.

"Levi! Levi! Wake up!" He groaned, but moved his legs. I figured at least his neck and back weren't broken. His chin was split open and pouring blood, as was his nose. I ran my hands over his collar bones, right arm, his ribs and legs. I didn't find anything obvious besides his left arm, which hung at a sickening angle.

"He's bad hurt. Kyle, find Kelly and have him get the wagon here in a hurry."

We loaded the still unconscious young drover into the wagon. Kelly whipped the mules into a trot, as Pecos held Levi to keep him from getting bounced too hard. Once we got him to where Zach had built a fire and made coffee, we lowered him to the ground and laid him on a tarp. We peeled off his wet clothes and cleaned all the raw spots, then gently redressed him in a pair of summer drawers. The split in his chin was full of grass and mud. I took advantage of his unconsciousness to clean it with soapy water followed by whiskey. His nose was broken, but easily shifted back into place. "Luke, your brother is hurt real bad. His face is gonna be black and blue in the mornin'. I'm gonna try to set his arm. I need you to find two stout, smooth branches as long as his arm and a clean flour sack."

When he got back, I showed him how to tear the sack into long strips. "Kelly, hold him down across his chest. Pecos, you hold him steady right above the elbow. I'll tell you when I'm gonna straighten it." I looked at it carefully. The skin wasn't broken. I got a firm grip around his wrist and just below the elbow. "Okay, now." I pulled hard and the bones snapped back into place. Levi's eyes flew open about that time and he yelled words his momma hadn't taught him. Luke held the branches in place, as Kyle handed me the torn strips. I tied them firmly into place. Kelly made a sling out of the rest of the flour sack. Levi was starting to holler pretty loud, so I measured him out a couple of tablespoons of laudanum. Within minutes, he was sleeping like a baby and we placed him in his bedroll.

"Aaron, that boy's hurt bad. Maybe it wouldn't hurt to lay off a couple of days to let him rest up some. After that, I think he can ride in the wagon."

Pecos joined in. "Them cattle ran off ten pounds of taller. It wouldn't hurt them to fatten up a couple of days."

"Alright. We'll set up here. Luke, you watch your brother close."

_____

The fresh beef was a rare treat. Kelly had grilled the steaks over the coals. Sweet water bubbled in a small stream. We made use of it for bathing and washing our clothes. There was a deep place downstream where the boys caught enough fish for a meal.

Luke came running up. "Come quick. Levi's passin' blood!"

"Levi, how bad is it?"

"About the color of plum jelly."

"Any blood clots in it?"

"Some. Is it bad?"

"It's not good. It means you got banged up inside as bad as outside. We're gonna give you enough water to float a Yankee iron-clad. You don't get up without someone helpin' you."

As I consulted Kelly about what to do, Kyle loped up, stopping the required distance from the wagon. "There's another herd comin' up the trail behind us. Their point man is headin' this way."

I climbed on my horse and rode out to meet him with Kyle.

"Mornin'! Name's A. B. Blocker from Texas. Folks call me Ab. You look like Texas drovers. I got a little set of steers we're drivin' to Kansas. Don't want to crowd you none."

"Aaron Turner, Limestone County, Texas. We got a herd of about fourteen hundred head goin' to Kansas, too. Got a man hurt bad in a stampede, so we stopped a while to let him heal up. You can drive past us; he's hurt too bad to leave yet. Had a couple of steers go down we had to butcher. We got fresh beef if your bunch would take supper with us."

"That sounds mighty fine to me, Bolivar. Would your boys help us keep the herds apart?"

"Sounds good."

"See you at supper."

Kelly acted about half put out for cookin' for extra folks, but this was just considered good trail manners, and he knew it. Sometimes Ol' Biscuit just liked to grumble a little. He cooked up fried beef steak, beans, biscuits and gravy, plus a huge blackberry cobbler for dessert.

Ab was good company. The man could sure talk and had plenty of good tales to tell. I think he was stretchin' the blanket quite a bit, but that made the stories that much better. "Bolivar, that's as good a supper as I've had in a long time. You can come cook for the Blocker outfit any time."

"My names Kelly, but they call me Biscuit. You want some more coffee? It's Arbuckle's."

"Thanks, Bolivar. I believe I do. How's your hurt drover doin'?"

"Split his chin, busted his left arm and passin' blood, but I think he'll live."

"Well, tell young Bolivar I'll be prayin'. 'The prayer of a righteous man availeth much.' But I reckon the Lord will hear an old reprobate like me, too."

"Ab, do you call everybody 'Bolivar'?"

"Everybody but my mother. That way I don't have to remember names."

We laughed, swapped lies and shared a jug until the moon was far up. That man could talk the ears off a donkey.

———

Levi gradually got better over the next two days. We rigged a hammock inside the wagon to cushion his ride. We were one man short on our rotation, but Kelly turned Zach loose to ride Levi's night guard. He was a punchy little kid.

The Dover Stage Station had certainly noted the passing of Blocker's herd. "Which of you fellas is Bolivar? He said to tell you howdy." We all raised our hands. "We got news about Injun troubles you Texans might want to know. The Kiowa under Satanta murdered a bunch of teamsters on the road between Fort Griffin and Fort Richardson at a place called Sand Creek. Killed seven of 'em and roasted one alive on a wagon tongue. They're callin' it the Sand Creek Massacre. General Sherman hisself was ridin' on an inspection tour and came within a whisker of being caught by Satanta. The Kiowa chased him and his escort all the way to Fort Griffin."

"Wish it was him they roasted." Pecos smiled.

"Maybe they'd do us a favor and barbeque Governor Davis, too." Kelly added.

"Mister, are they receiving cattle at Caldwell yet?"

"Yessir, I guess Blocker's herd will be the first if he don't talk his cattle to death."

"You got a doctor here?"

"Yeah. He's a retired army doctor. Not half bad, either. His office is behind the post office."

We took Levi in the small office. The doctor wore the blue coat of a Union medical officer. He greeted us, washed his hands and started removing the splint. "Who set this forearm?"

"I did, Captain."

"How'd you know I was a Captain? Were you in the war?"

"Yessir. Long enough to recognize a Yankee officer when I see one. I got sent to Camp Stephen Douglas. I worked in the hospital."

"Camp Douglas was a pretty bad place. I'm retired now. I don't mind treatin' Johnny Rebs as long as they pay in Yankee dollars." He smiled and put us at ease. "You did a good job patching him up. I'll replace the splint with a plaster cast. Mind helping me?"

He carefully applied the plaster soaked cotton strips and formed a nice above-the-elbow cast. "It will set up pretty quickly. Don't mess with it for a couple of hours. You can take it off in Caldwell. That'll be three dollars, please."

After a few days, Levi's pain was a lot better. He thought he could handle the team. Kelly and Zach hitched the wagon, and Kelly rode his big horse on the flank until time to stop for supper. When we got to the Arkansas, he turned the reins over to Kelly and perched on the seat next to him. The crossing was the easiest one yet. I guess the way our luck had been so far, it was about time for a break.

Once we were across, Kelly took over Levi's duties at flank again. It was a strange last few days of the drive. Kelly worked as a drover; Levi drove the wagon and helped Zach take over the cooking with advice from Kelly. They all showed to be pretty good sports about it. We made it fine, if somewhat out of order, to Caldwell.

Caldwell was rough as a corncob. Abilene had rough edges, but Caldwell was rough all the way to the bone. This was the end of the line for the Caldwell spur of the Atchison, Topeka and Santa Fe Railroad. The town was crawling with railroad workers. The buildings were mostly tents with wood floors, even the bank. A huge safe stood in the middle of the bare floor surrounded by four heavily armed men. The stock pens were well laid out and had only been used by Blocker's herd. I found Joseph McCoy's agent. "Where's Blocker? He got here ahead of us."

"Yeah, he got here ahead of you, but his drovers got in a big fight with the railroad men. The sheriff tried to arrest them, but Ol' Ab pulled down the jail. He drove his cattle out of the pens and said he was going to Abilene. We're kinda glad to have a civilized bunch of drovers."

"They won't take much guff from those railroad men. These boys have fought Yankees, outlaws and Indians. They want to be left alone, but if anybody picks on 'em, they'll fight back hard. Think your sheriff can handle that?"

"Yeah, I do. I talked to the railroad receiving manager. He knows they missed a good opportunity with Ab Blocker. Your herd is three times as big. His men are restricted to camp west of town while you're here."

"I'd like to get myself and my men cleaned up before we go to the bank to settle up. You got one of those Chinese bathhouses, barber shop, and laundry?"

"Sure do, they're expecting you; my treat. Meet you at the bank before lunch?"

"Alright. Your tallies match mine?"

"We were off by one head, so I split the difference with you. That suit ya?"

"Fair enough, which way to the bathhouse?"

———————

This place was pretty much like the one in Abilene. By the time we got the trail grime scrubbed off, haircuts and shaves, our clothes were clean and dried. We let Levi soak his cast off. His arm was skinny, but looked pretty good.

We all walked down to the bank. I drew out enough in silver for everybody's pay and the expenses for the trip home. This bank was a branch of the Abilene bank. I didn't leave until I had a confirming telegram from the Cattleman's Bank in Waco that the funds had been transferred. The cattle sold for twenty-seven dollars a head plus the two dollar bonus for being the first herd, since Blocker's herd left.

Kelly and Zach restocked the wagon for the trip back. The boys and I did our usual shopping. New Stetsons and Levis were pretty popular. We had a big lunch at the only café in Caldwell. They served pancakes and syrup, pork chops with red-eye gravy, big tall biscuits, fresh butter, jam and coffee.

As a group, we didn't have anything against kicking up our heels at times, but we were ready to get home. We camped outside Caldwell that night and headed back to Texas the next morning. Levi was able to handle his horse, and we all got settled into our simple routine. Our crew was pretty boring. I think Matt and Pecos tossed back some scamper juice after lunch, and most of the others had a beer or sarsaparilla.

The trip back was troubled only by a few mild summer showers. We stopped at the Dover Stage Station. The station master had some news. "The army finally got tired of Satanta. They whipped the dog out of his war band and captured him. Had a trial and sent him off to Huntsville prison."

"That's sure enough good news. How are things in Texas?"

"Pretty good if you're colored or a carpetbagger. Pretty bad for old Rebs like you."

We headed down the trail and crossed the Red River back into Texas on August 10. For better or worse, it was home. We stopped at the store and checked the news and got Kelly some more tobacco. We kept the wagon heading south reaching Waco before the month was out. We took care of our business, said our good-byes and scattered to our homes. Pecos and I reached Groesbeck on September 1, 1871. It sure was good to see Momma and the family. I was even sort of glad to see Alice.

18

September 1871, Groesbeck, Limestone County, Texas

The Tide Turns

CONSERVATIVE REPUBLICANS were astonished at the unprecedented level of corruption in the Davis administration and legislature. Taxes had risen to shocking levels to support outlandish spending by their former allies, the Radical Republicans. Fully twenty-one percent of Texan's income went to state taxes. In September, the Conservative Republicans convened a taxpayers' meeting in Austin. They encouraged the previously ignored Democrats to join them. Since it was not a public election, old Confederates could address the assembly and vote on the non-binding resolutions. Ninety-four counties sent delegates. Among other issues, the meeting demanded elections be held in the fall of 1871 as required in the Constitution, not 1872 as legislated by Davis. In response, General Reynolds and Governor Davis organized huge turbulent protests by Negroes in Austin to intimidate the taxpayers' meeting. If anything, it galvanized their resolve to end the tyranny that had fallen upon Texas. Newspapers across the state, except those on Davis' payroll, emboldened by the meeting, took up the cry for fairness, freedom and the restoration of democracy. These papers were met with broken windows and vandalism by the State Police. Davis finally consented to elections in the fall of 1871.

———————

Pistol shots rang out loudly in the crisp night air in downtown Groesbeck. "Marcus, you hear that?"

"Yep. You and Pecos get your guns."

As we stepped out the door of Marcus' house, two more shots pierced the night. Dogs barked, mules brayed and horses pranced and nickered. The shots had come from Main Street. It was faster to run there on foot, as our horses were in the stable. Rounding the corner onto Main Street, we saw four black State Policemen reloading their guns over the lifeless body of an apparently unarmed white man. One wore sergeant's stripes. His voice boomed out, slurred with liquor. "All you crackers hear me! This town's gonna be runnin' with white men's blood by mornin'!" He and his companions turned to the nearest store and kicked the door open. They demolished the small store, finishing by throwing a chair through the window. We kept under cover as they re-entered the street. We could see other armed citizens peering around corners and from under porches. Men with rifles appeared on the second floor gallery of the hotel. Seeing new targets for their rage, the black men unleashed drunken pistol shots at the hotel. The men on the gallery were stone-cold sober and returned well aimed shots at the murderers, wounding one. "We gonna kill all you crackers!"

They kicked their way into the stone city office building and barricaded themselves inside. Groesbeck's mayor, Elijah Zadek, urged the town to arm themselves. As a posse organized down the street, the four men managed to slip out the back door.

They made their way to a nearby Negro settlement. Once they were there, they raised an angry mob and headed for Groesbeck. The officers were easily distinguished by their uniforms. Pecos dropped to one knee and took careful aim. His Henry roared and one of the policemen went down, a huge hole in his chest. "That darkie ain't gonna kill no more white men!" He swung his rifle and squeezed off another shot into the surging crowd. The bullet dropped another man in uniform. By now, Marcus and I, along with a dozen other men, poured shots into the angry milling group of Negroes. The two remaining policemen disappeared into the crowd, as they began to turn and run for their homes.

Marcus guarded his house next to Mother's cabin where I was stationed. The heavy wooden shutters were closed, the doors barred, and both Mother and I held loaded guns. Pecos took the more dangerous job of guarding Marcus' tavern. Bonfires fed by angry black men were built in the roads, guarding every approach to the Negro settlement. It was a long sleepless night.

By morning, a company of colored cavalry arrived commanded by an arrogant redheaded Irish captain. Limestone County was placed under martial law. The posse was disbanded. No effort was made to find the surviving policemen. Armed troopers kept their carbines trained on the white citizens at the funeral of the white victim.

Two days later, there was a pounding of hooves in front of the cabin. The Irish captain strode up to the porch. He spat tobacco juice on Mother's porch. "Come out of the house unarmed. Now!"

"Why should we, Billy Yank?"

"Because if ya don't we'll burn the house down around your treasonous ears and shoot anyone that comes out!"

Pecos and I stepped out on the porch. "All of ya, dammit!" Mother and Alice stood behind us. "Governor Davis has issued an executive order for a fine to be assessed on all property owners in Limestone County of three percent of the appraised value of the property. If the fine is not paid within forty-eight hours, the property will be forfeited to the state."

"You gonna give me a receipt for the fine?"

Before I saw it coming, he hit me in the mouth hard enough to knock me down, then spit tobacco on my shirt. "That's all the receipt you'll be gettin', ya Rebel trash. It'll be fifteen dollars, you treasonous vermin."

"In the house." I mumbled through swollen lips.

"Go with him, Private. I don't want him gettin' a gun." A Negro private followed me into the house. His glare dared me to try something. I counted out fifteen silver dollars and walked back to the porch. I threw the money at the captain's feet. He smashed my head with the barrel of his revolver. When I woke up, they were gone. My hatred for Governor Davis, Yankee troops, State Policemen, and carpetbaggers was glowing like hot coals deep inside.

November brought cooler weather, rock bottom cotton and cattle prices and an election. Several seats in the state legislature were coming open. Thousands of Texans flooded the polls. I was a Confederate veteran, as was Pecos, so we couldn't vote. But just about any man over the age of twenty-one who had not served headed to the polls. They raised their hands and swore the Iron Clad Oath. The local election boards sensed the hostility of the voters and didn't question their eligibility to vote. Marcus voted at Groesbeck. Governor Davis used the State Police and Federal troops to try to intimidate the potential voters, but they were having none of it. Democrats won every open seat. Davis had thousands of votes thrown out, and he threw out the entire set of votes from Limestone, Brazos, Bowie and Marion counties.

The United States Assistant Attorney General, even though he was a Republican, indicted Governor Davis for election fraud. The matter was resolved in typical Reconstruction manner. The gentleman was immediately removed from office by President Grant. His replacement "lost" all the evidence against Davis, who was acquitted. Davis had dodged the political bullet, but his own Radical Republicans initiated an investigation into the condition of the state's finances. The commission found that in spite of staggering taxes, Texas was on the verge of bankruptcy. They accused Davis of "reckless diversion of public funds for private benefit."

The tyrant's own party was growing weary of him. His former allies, the Conservative Republicans, despised him, and found common cause with the resurging Democrats. We all sensed that his days were numbered. Hope began to grow that Texas might return to normalcy soon.

19

**March 1872, Turner Ranch, North Fork of Pecan Bayou,
Texas frontier**

The Prodigal Returns

"LOOK AT 'EM, PECOS. THAT'S the best calf crop we ever had."

"Yep. Those Devon bulls really shine up those ol' longhorns."

We had sent word for our trail hands to meet up on our growing ranch on Pecan Bayou. Matt and Jake Dawson, Luke and Levi Carter and Kyle Shepard had ridden down together. Kelly Webb brought his little boy, Jake, with Zach Barton when he had picked up our chuck wagon and mules. To avoid confusion, the two Jakes were known as Jake and Little Jake. Jake Dawson was now fifteen, five foot eight, and didn't shave yet, but he could hold up his own with about anybody on the place.

"With cattle prices so low this year, I'm gonna hold all the market cattle over a year to fatten on grass. We got enough for four times as many cattle, so even if it's a dry year we should be alright."

"You're the boss." Pecos grinned. The hands had pushed the herd up into a large meadow across the creek from the dugout. They were kept busy all day sorting out

---

calves to brand and castrate. They would rope them by the back feet and drag them to the fire where I would flank them. While Little Jake branded them, Kelly castrated the bull calves. Zach notched a half-moon out of the tops of both ears.

Pecos had reserved four nice cross bull calves. They appeared to be out of our older Shorthorn cross cows and the Devon bulls. "What do ya think?"

"They're long bodied, got heavy muscles, seem gentle. I guess these are the best young bulls we've ever raised. Let's brand and ear-notch these ourselves. We don't want the boys to get excited and castrate 'em."

"Kelly fixed a big supper of calf fries, biscuits, beans and gravy with an apricot cobbler. It made my aches and pains feel better. Our herd was growing in numbers and quality. The pasture was as good as I had ever seen it. For the first time, I didn't see any buffalo. That made me think of Noah. I wondered if he was even alive. The Cheyenne along the Republican River didn't like buffalo hunters at all. I had heard stories about the plains there being filled with naked, rotting buffalo carcasses. It seemed like a terrible waste to slaughter an animal just for the hide and let the meat go to waste. But there was good money for the hides and it was Noah's business and not mine. I slept well that night. Our work there was done, and we headed to our other home in Limestone County the next day.

Matt had grown into every bit as good a hand as Pecos, and better than me. When it came to shoeing a horse, he and Pecos were both top-notch. Jake was the punchiest kid in Texas. He wasn't afraid of anything or anybody, and rode like a Comanche. Kyle was long and lean. He handled himself like a grown man. Luke and Levi had both grown, and were still growing, but they got to be better hands each year. Zach Barton would go back to his job as wrangler and cook's helper on our next drive, but this trip gave him a chance to show us he had the makings of a good hand. Of course, Biscuit was always good company and a good cook. Little Jake had given all he had every day until he fell over asleep in his clothes at night. He wasn't ready for the trail yet, but he had lots of "try" in him. It was a good bunch of men and boys and I was proud they rode for me.

Kelly dropped the wagon off at Mother's place in Groesbeck. Pecos and I had ridden back with him. I noticed a strange horse in the end stall. "I wonder who that black gelding belongs to."

"He's mine." I turned to see Noah standing in the barn door. He was only twenty-four, but looked older. They had been hard years for all of us.

"Noah!" I sprinted to give him a hug. "When did you get here?"

"Last week. The huntin' has played out on the Republican. We done real good, though. I got half a dozen Studebaker wagons and plenty of good strong mules. I can't say much good about the men that work for me. They got lice; stink like buffalo, lie, drink, and gamble. But they work hard enough and know how to handle their guns and skinnin' knives. We get plenty of company from the northern Cheyenne. I left everything up at Bent's Fort on the Arkansas in Colorado territory. We'll be headin' that way before winter."

"I'm mighty glad to see ya. You come home for a visit?"

"Well, yes. I came home for you to meet my wife. She grew up at Teague over in Freestone County. Her name is Mary. You'll like her.

Mary was tall and slender and beautiful. She had auburn hair and blue eyes that sparkled with friendship. We really enjoyed getting to know her. It was obvious she and Noah were deeply in love. Before we went to bed that night, Noah suggested I come with him to check his horse. I raised my eyebrows, but followed out to the barn. I expected to hear that perhaps Mary had been pregnant when they married or something, but I wasn't prepared for what Noah told me. "Aaron, when Mary was fifteen, she got raped by a Yankee officer. She got pregnant, but the baby died. Her parents were so ashamed, they turned her out of the house. She ran away from home and wound up in Ogallala working in a whorehouse. I met her and fell in love with her. I don't know all the places she has worked. She goes out on the wagons with me where I can protect her. She'll be livin' in a tent on the plains, but as long as we're together, she doesn't complain. She has a good heart, and I love her." Noah had tears rolling down his weathered face.

"Noah, she's a beautiful woman who loves you, and you love her. I'll love her because of you. All that other doesn't matter. I'll never tell anyone, even Mother."

"If something happens to me, I want to know you'll protect her and make sure she's taken care of."

"I promise, big brother. I owe it to you. But I'd rather you be around to take care of her yourself."

———————

A new kind of Yankee officer had come to the Texas frontier the previous summer. Colonel Ranald S. Mackenzie was a West Point graduate who had distinguished himself as a cavalry officer in the late war. He led from the front, having been wounded six times in battle. When he had come to Texas, he had been given command of the United States Fourth Cavalry, headquartered at Fort Richardson. As most of the troops in Texas, these were Negro troops led by white officers. They had been a ragtag undisciplined unit until Mackenzie took command. He shaped them into a force capable of dealing with Comanche, Kiowa and Apache. He trained them in new tactics to be more effective in Indian warfare. He effectively linked Fort Richardson to Fort Griffin to Fort Phantom Hill to Fort Concho. Mounted patrols met each other half way, and then returned. The various forts formed a cohesive line of defense, resupply and bases of operation for offensive campaigns against the Plains Indians.

In the summer of 1872, Mackenzie launched what was known as the Llano Estacado Campaign, from the Spanish for "staked plains." Mounted units began to systematically explore and map the treeless plains, so they knew where canyons gave shelter, springs gave water, and temporary playa lakes might appear after a rain. They learned that the Comanchero traders from New Mexico were key players in supplying the Comanche with weapons and trade goods. His troops shadowed their wagons and high-wheeled carts to hidden places unknown to white men. The Comanche called their new foes "buffalo soldiers" for their curly hair and dark skins. The name stuck. The actions of Colonel Mackenzie and his buffalo soldiers slowly started to make life a little safer all along the frontier.

———

Fall found Pecos and me returning to Groesbeck after tending our cattle all summer. They had prospered. We closed up the dugout and headed back to Limestone County. Campaigning for the national elections was in full swing. Marcus kept newspapers at his tavern which we thumbed through.

"Pecos, get a load of this campaign ad: 'U.S. Grant. Just and Honest.' I wish I had a wagonload of that to plow into Mamma's garden. I'd trust a fox in a hen house more than that ol' snake. We seen what kinda justice we get here in Texas from him. I doubt the ol' drunk has got an honest bone in his body."

"I got ya beat. Here's one for Governor Davis: 'Edmund J. Davis. Personal integrity and incorruptibility.'" We all had to laugh at that one. We knew firsthand what Davis was all about."

No Radical Republicans came to campaign in Limestone County. I guess they knew it would be a lost cause. In the cities, the State Police tried to intimidate candidates, newspapers and voters. For President, the Democrats ran newspaper publisher and businessman Horace Greeley. As far as we knew, the only thing he had done to commend him was his often quoted slogan: "Go west, young man." The main thing that really mattered was that he was not Grant.

In Texas, Greeley easily carried the state over Grant, but nationally our old enemy was re-elected. State legislative seats that came open fell largely to Democrats. For the first time since the start of congressional Reconstruction began, the Democrats held a majority in both the Texas House and the Senate. Governor Davis would find himself presiding over a very hostile legislature when they were seated in January. Maybe things were starting to look up. There was a whisper of hope in the winter wind, a promise of better days to come.

20

Redemption

THE THIRTEENTH LEGISLATURE was seated in Austin. We called it the "Rebel Legislature." It would serve for a very short time, but it had a tremendous impact on Texas. They quickly acted to undo the worst of the Radical Republican agenda. The governor's ability to declare martial law and force citizen into the militia was abolished. The State Police were eliminated. The governor's right to appoint or vacate all elected and appointed offices in the state was abolished, as was the printing law. Davis vetoed the new legislation which was then passed over his veto. Many conservative Republicans joined the Democrats. The now former State Policemen quickly disappeared before an angry public could seek justice for their brutality. Office holders who had been appointed by Davis either left their office vacant and fled the state or renounced their former leader.

Celebrations and bonfires broke out all across the state as word spread of the demise of Davis' power. Fairness and the rule of law and democracy were to be restored. The Iron Clad Oath was set aside for the earlier

Oath of Loyalty. This meant that former Confederate soldiers like me could vote, hold office and serve on juries. There was to be an election for governor in December. Richard Coke, a former Confederate officer was now eligible to hold office and was quickly nominated by the Democratic Party. He had commanded a company in our regiment. Captain Tyus, Noah, Pecos and I knew him well.

Governor Davis had one more cow pie to step in. He was pressured by do-gooders in Washington to release Satanta from prison. He issued a pardon and he was set free. The wolf was loose among the sheep. He immediately raised a war band and began to raid fiercely along the Red River. Many Texans would die before he would be returned to prison where he committed suicide.

———

"Pecos! They're here! Get your horse."

We galloped the short distance to the Groesbeck General Store. We tied our horses at the rail and ran inside. Waiting for us on the counter was a box containing two Colt Model 72 breech loading revolvers in .44-40. They had a cylinder which loaded brass cartridges from the rear. They had hard rubberized grips with a rearing colt on them. Next to them was a pair of Winchester Model 73 breech loading lever action rifles in .44-40. They used the same shells as the pistols. The walnut stock had a hand-rubbed linseed oil finish. They were beautiful. We paid for the guns and a case of cartridges and went back home to try them out.

The mechanisms on the pistols were smooth and crisp, made like a fine watch. They had 4 5/8 inch barrels and an unbelievable natural balance. It didn't take long to find that they were good shooting guns, the finest I had ever owned. The rifles were just as nice. The center-fire brass cartridges were much more potent then the rimfire Henry loads. The rifles were dead on to shoot.

"If we had these, we would have won the war!"

"Nah. The Yankees would have had them, too."

———

Pecos, Marcus and I rode to the polling place at city hall in Groesbeck. There was such a crowd, we had to tie the horses at Marcus' tavern two blocks away. It took a while to get certified to vote. Marcus swore I had been born in 1850. Pecos wasn't sure what year he was born, but thought it was 1848. We took the Loyalty Oath and each paid a poll tax of a dollar to vote. There were black men there from the Freedmen's Bureau passing out silver dollars for the poll tax to all the colored men, telling them to vote for Davis. It sure wasn't a hard choice for me. I voted for Richard Coke.

We walked over to Marcus' tavern, which wasn't allowed to serve alcohol on Election Day. They did a big business in stew and cornbread, though. The polls closed at sunset and the poll watchers from all three parties watched as the votes were counted. Coke swept Limestone County. As the night wore on, the telegraph office buzzed with results from other counties. By midnight, it appeared Coke had carried the state by a landslide, but the official tallies would be a few days coming. Inauguration Day was set for January 19, 1874.

_____

The Fourteenth Legislature was set to begin on Inauguration Day. Governor Davis had declared the December elections null and void due to voter fraud. He appealed to the Texas Supreme Court that the elections had not been scheduled at the time and date specified in the Texas Constitution. In fact, they had not. They had been set by Davis to try to retain power. The Justices, all Davis appointees, agreed with Davis.

Captain Coke sent word that Davis was trying to steal the election. Captain Tyus had received a telegram asking him to gather armed men he trusted and get to Austin quickly. He sent for me and our hands. We were to pack light, ride fast and come armed. Kelly, Matt and Jake, Luke and Levi, Kyle, Zach, Pecos and I answered the call. We got to the Captain's ranch January 10. Kelly had come thundering in on his draft horse. We carried rifles, pistols, bedrolls and war bags. The Captain had two pack mules loaded with provisions. He rode a fine jet black Thoroughbred stallion and wore his Confederate uniform. He unfurled our old Bonnie Blue flag and gave it to Zach to carry. Counting the Captain, there were ten of us. We crossed the Brazos on the cold morning of January 11. We pushed our horses hard all day and found ourselves in Austin well after dark.

We found a place along the Colorado River about a mile south of the Capital building to camp. Captain Tyus went immediately to report to Richard Coke. Before the night was over, there were hundreds of men, ex-Confederates, old Texas Rangers and common ranch hands along the river.

———

On January 12, 1874, Governor Davis telegraphed that he needed the Federal troops in and near Austin to re-establish martial law. Grant declined and sent orders Federal troops were to stand down unless attacked. Hundreds of us marched north along Congress Avenue to the south doors to the Capital. The doors were locked. The last of the Davis supporters and his bodyguard retreated to the basement. Davis barricaded himself in his office. We battered down the door and locked all the exits from the basement.

Over the next few days, more Texans flocked to Austin until reports estimated there were three thousand armed men. Governor Davis ordered the Travis County Rifles to come to his aid. Instead, they armed themselves and joined Coke's camp.

On January 15, a huge mob of black men arrived in Austin from Houston. Davis had the State Armory opened and the mob armed. One by one, and in small groups, they were persuaded to lay down their weapons and go home. The men who had paid them to come had already fled Austin.

A Yankee carpetbagger officer named Degress and a handful of desperate Radical Republicans wheeled a nine-pounder cannon to fire directly at the well guarded south door of the capital building. The gun failed to fire because Coke's men had thought to spike the gun's touch hole with a brass nail, making it impossible to fire. They threw down their weapons and surrendered.

January 19, 1874, dawned on our camp on the Colorado. Men filed onto Congress Avenue from every direction. Rough and tough Brigadier General John "Rip" Ford, tall, straight, red-faced and grim, led the armed body north to the Capital. Texas flags and the Bonnie Blue flag fluttered in countless numbers among the determined armed men. They sang "The Yellow Rose of Texas" as they marched. However, no Federal troops appeared to bar their way. The Capital doors were thrown open. The rats hiding in the basement were run out. The doors to the Governor's office were battered down. Edmund J. Davis, the tyrant of Texas, escaped by climbing unceremoniously out a window.

Rip Ford opened the proceedings and swore-in each new and retuning member of the House and Senate. The assembly was declared duly sworn-in and called to order. Richard Coke was then administered the oath of office and the Fourteenth Legislature was in session.

He thanked those who had come to his aid and gave us leave to return to our homes. As we gathered our things and saddled our horses, Captain Tyus walked over to Pecos and me. "Texas is finally free again, boys, like a phoenix rising from the ashes of war and Reconstruction. We are finally free."

Epilogue

TEXAS HAD BEEN ALMOST physically untouched by the War Between the States. But many young Texans had marched away never to return. King Cotton had been dethroned, and the Texas economy had been in shambles.

Reconstruction was a brutal injustice inflicted with deliberate malice on proud Texans. But from the ashes of war and Reconstruction, Texas and Texans rose up and rebuilt their state and their lives.

The hardy longhorns were gathered from cane breaks, river bottoms and wide prairies. They were driven by the tens of thousands to Northern markets hungry for Texas beef. These intrepid Texas drovers traded cattle for Yankee dollars that flooded back into the suffering Texas economy. The impact of these drovers and their cattle cannot be underestimated in the recovery of Texas from the ruin of war.

Aaron Lloyd Turner and his family literally saw their home reduced to ashes in the violence of Reconstruction. They sold their land and moved farther west. Their early ranching enterprise on the tributaries of Pecan Bayou would one day become the center of their new home in Callahan and Taylor Counties.

Glossary

Calf fries: fried bull testicles

Chouse: to chase roughly

Cimarrone: outlaw

Double eagle: a twenty dollar gold piece

Found (n): an old term for food and lodging

Foxfire: an electrical phenomena observed during times of electrical storms causing a yellow-green (also sometimes reported to be blue) light seen outlining animals, people, and objects; it is sometimes associated with a hissing or humming sound; also known as St. Elmo's fire

Hard tack: dense tough dough baked into cracker-like cakes; if kept dry, they could last for months or years

Hock: lower leg of an animal, roughly equivalent to an ankle

Hollow horn: a folk medicine diagnosis for a variety of ailments in cattle, cured by sawing off all or part of the horns

Jingle bob: 1. the ear of a cow which has been split horizontally to show ownership; 2. A weighted metal clapper on spurs used to make a metallic sound

Mexia: me-hay'-ah; the county seat of Limestone County, Texas

Montague County: mon'-tag; a county in north central Texas on the Red River

Moss back, mossy horn: a term for an old animal

Punchy: a tough cowhand with good skills and attitude

Rawhide (n): untanned cowhide; (v) to joke coarsely

Remuda: ree moo' dah; a herd of horses

Segundo: second in charge, literally, the second

Single tree: the part of a draft animal's equipment used to fasten the animal to the tongue of the wagon or plow

Soogans: sou'-gans; bedroll or blankets; multiple alternate spellings

Stag: a male bovine castrated after adulthood

Steer: a male bovine castrated before adulthood

Stretching the blanket: a phrase which implies exaggeration for the purpose of improving upon a story

Tallow: beef fat; could be eaten as a poor substitute for butter, or for making candles

Wrangler: hand in charge of the remuda

Wreck pan: large pan or bucket for receiving dirty dishes

Suggested Reading

Abbott, E. C. *We Pointed them North*. Norman. University of Oklahoma
Press. 1939

Campbell, Randolph B. *Gone to Texas: a History of the Lone Star State*. New
York. Oxford University Press. 2003

Capps, Benjamin. *The Trail to Ogallala*. Fort Worth. TCU Press. 1985

Dobie, J. Frank. *Cow People*. Austin. University of Texas Press. 1964

Dobie, J. Frank. *The Longhorns*. Austin. University of Texas Press. 1985

Fehrenbach, T.R. *Lone Star: A History of Texas and Texans*. New York:
Collier Books. 1968

Newcomb, W.W., Junior. *The Indians of Texas*. Austin. University of Texas
Press. 1985

Genealogy

Thomas Turner, Ireland, circa 1732; died SC, 1796 = Priscella Alexander, Ireland

Thomas Turner, Jr., Marlboro Co., SC, 1751; died Marlboro Co., SC, 1822 = Rebekah unknown

Aaron Turner, Marlboro Co., SC, 1783; died, Leon Co., TX, 1851 = Nancy King, GA

Aaron Lloyd Turner, Leon Co., TX, 1850; died Terry Co., TX, 1939 = Ella Fisher, Limestone Co., TX

John K. Turner, Taylor Co., TX, 1890; died Gaines Co., TX 1964 = Effie Smith, MO

Aaron Lynn Turner, Gaines Co., TX, 1931; = Doris Alene Combs, Madison Co., AR

Stephen Lynn Turner, Washington, Co., AR, 1957 =Roberta Lyles, East Baton Rouge Parrish, LA

Melissa Turner, Lubbock Co., TX, 1984 = Dustin DeBusk, TX

Aaron Lyles Turner, Hale Co., TX, 1988 = Sarah Robinson, TX

www.ingramcontent.com/pod-product-compliance
Lightning Source LLC
Chambersburg PA
CBHW011355010726

47494CB00008B/2334